Stefanie

Warren Pierce

◆ FriesenPress

One Printers Way
Altona, MB R0G 0B0
Canada

www.friesenpress.com

ISBN
978-1-5255-9338-3 (Hardcover)
978-1-5255-9337-6 (Paperback)
978-1-5255-9339-0 (eBook)

1. Fiction, Coming Of Age

Distributed to the trade by The Ingram Book Company

Acknowledgements

In no particular order . . .

Thomas Hargrove, Bruce King, Nick Johnson, Gregg
Goldston, and Noe Zavala: Mentors of my artistic education.

Geoffrey Infeld: Remember the dust.

Jane Austen, Richard Curtis, Nora Ephron, Sheri Reynolds,
J.R.R. Tolkien, Stephen King, Stieg Larsson: Inspiration.

Mimi Zungri Anderson: Ouch!

The State Street & Sacramento Ballets: Giving me a chance.

Lisa Santos Laubacher, Nina Baratova, and Jasper: Just for
being you!

Toby Roye: Midnight teenage rooftop escapades.

Carla [?] (CHS 1984), Jillian Isley Morgan: Zoe.

Stephen King: *On Writing*.

Francis Hoar Trucksess (G-ma): Her gift of exaggeration.

Jim Johnson @accenthelp: Assistance with dialects.

Dr Seuss: My pun-ish sense of humour.

Katie Kelley: For being there.

Nastya Pavlenko: Assistance with Ukrainian and photo model for Stefanie.

Ellis Kopier and Stephanie Gille: Assistance with Dutch.

Roberta Robledo and Adriana Hoyos: Assistance with Spanish.

Johan Renvall, Gary McKenzie, Constance Dominguez, Lisi Caren Gotaas Walsh, Sylvie Guillem: Your art.

Yarosh Bohdana: Photos.

Maxwell Maltz's quote from *Psycho-Cybernetics* used with permission.

Special thanks to Nastya Pavlenko: Who helped me more than she knew.

Without you . . . this story would not have been possible.

An Interlude of Stefanie
Preface

I do not write stories. I did not write this one—not really—not the good stuff, at least. That might sound like an odd thing for a writer to say, but I stand by it.

I was fortunate to simply be present when the writing came and used me as its vehicle. Of course, you will see my prints in the forced passages, the stubborn word I refused to delete, the paragraph that doesn't quite work, but for me, whatever the medium—be it dance, choreography, or writing—I do best by getting out of the way and allowing the process to flow: to loose the muse, so to speak (I bet you thought either "lose the muse" or "loose the moose," didn't you?—funny how minds work).

Beginning life as a ballet-themed romance, it eventually evolved to become a "better late than never" coming-of-age story—as well as a story of love: love in the romantic sense most certainly, but also the deep love of genuine friendships, love for flawed mentors and of odd pairings, a parent's inviolable love for their children, love of art and animals, love required to endure an annoying acquaintance, perhaps even the concern one can still feel for an old lover, and, without a doubt, no small measure of tough love.

Vocabulary Notes

Dutch profanity makes much use of both disease terminology and bodily areas . . . and Stefanie makes much use of Dutch profanity.

A "dance belt" is not a "belt" but a "jock" for male dancers.

Australian diminutives include:
- brekkie = breakfast
- pickie = photo/picture
- Chrissie = Christmas

The Bolshoi is a major Russian ballet company.

George Balanchine was the Director of New York City Ballet and an influential twentieth-century choreographer.

Ballet companies are often referred to by their acronyms: i.e., American Ballet Theater is called ABT.

Corps de ballet: The body of the ballet (not soloists or principals).

"Flicking a V": a sort of reverse peace sign, palm facing signer, is the English equivalent of "flipping the bird."

"Slag" is an English equivalent of slut

"Snog" = Kiss

"Pavlovian" may refer to salivating animals, but it also may be a reference to Anna Pavlova, a famous ballerina known for her highly arched feet.

Ballon (ba-láwn) is a dancer's ability to "cling in the air."

I've tried to avoid technical dance terminology, though in the interest of phrasing, sometimes it was unavoidable.

"Turning" is a casual way of referring to pirouettes.

"RP" stands for "received pronunciation": A non-regional educated British accent; also called "BBC English."

"Estuary" is a somewhat umbrella-like term for a range of British accents falling somewhere between Cockney and RP.

Broad Australian (or Broad Aussie) is a working class Australian accent.

For Nastya

I am only resolved to act in that manner, which will, in my own opinion, constitute my happiness, without reference to you, or to any person so wholly unconnected with me.

—Elizabeth Bennet

My dearest Eliza—what constitutes happiness?

—Margin note, Dec. 11

Entrée

. . . Airports can be such desolate lonely places.

1

Stefanie Janssen

Friday, December 13th

It was well into December when I decided to leave the temperate climes of Santa Barbara and, at my mother's insistence, accompany her on a weekend trip to Seattle. She was travelling to attend a conference. I was coming, I suppose . . . because I needed some distance from my current drama.

His name was Marcus.

Marcus had recently proposed to me, and while this turn of events was not entirely unexpected, I'd told him I needed a few days to think it over.

A few days, and a few (even) less-than-usual nights' sleep.

He insisted I take the enormously large engagement ring he purchased along with me, and to my discredit, I had. I had been toying with it—and what it represented—the entire flight.

Why is it that one feels so dreadfully out of place while flying?

3

I'd find myself slipping the ring on and wearing it for a while . . .

You have your life, your story, and there is a certain comfort in that—a certain familiarity, at least.

Seeing how the ring looked—how it felt—before again replacing it back in its case.

And when you find yourself confined in a metal tube with complete strangers . . . the relevance of your own life seems suddenly at a vast distance.

While Mum busied herself with documents in the seat next to me, I gazed out the window of the plane and waited for the ring to do its job.

And though aware of your destination, you somehow feel you've lost your way.

I wanted the ring to work its magic and convince me with its charms. So far, however, the defining emotional thrust I was hoping for remained absent.

And isn't it rather unsettling—or even surreal? As if the once-steadfast rules of life no longer apply, and upon landing, the only thing you will have ever had in common with these people was a brief time shared in a metal tube.

* * *

While I offered to pay for an Uber to the hotel, Mum—never one for "needless extravagance," as she put it—insisted on taking the light rail.

And so it was, from one metal tube we emerged only to board another.

Different tubes, different strangers, different stories. This time, however, being below the clouds, the greyness only contributed to my vacancy.

There was really little choice but to marry Marcus, of course. I knew this, and my hesitation was perceived by all as nothing but good form. And why not? Marcus was a wonderful man, with almost (but not quite) movie-star good looks—character actor, certainly—and not to mention wealthy.

Arriving at the hotel with no time to unpack, Mum was "notes in hand," getting prepared to give a lecture. The fact she was in a hurry didn't stop her from giving me one last admonition on her way out.

"Downtown is right here, Stefanie," she declared. "Don't wallow about in the room all day. Go out and explore. Have something to eat, and we'll meet back here later this evening. Remember, Stefanie—Seattle awaits you."

Despite nearly thirty years living in the UK and America, Mum's somewhat domineering manor and Dutch accent remained her most prevalent features.

How had I let myself be talked into such an excursion? Certainly, there were other places I might have gone to have "my think"—places with actual sunlight, for instance. I suppose I had seen it as a way to reconnect with Mum, with whom I've had a slightly contentious relationship since . . . *Well, since forever, really.*

At nineteen, I moved from the UK to accept a principal

position at Capital City Ballet in California: a smaller but well-respected company.

Better to be the big fish in a small pond, I reasoned, than just another medium-sized fish in the ocean.

That being said, the allure of having an ocean's distance between us—free from Mum's subjugation, however well intended ("love-jugation," as I had come to think of it)—was undeniably an added bonus.

So, when after less than a year's parole from Mum's purview, she casually mentioned her business was expanding to the US, and she was hopping across the pond to oversee start-up operations, I actually cried a little.

Of course, she didn't say she would be setting up shop in Capital City—she didn't need to. It was a given.

Listen, I'm being too hard on her. I don't want to begin this way. I love my mother, and while a force to be reckoned with, I have never wanted for anything, and she has been a positive driving force in my life. And she loves me; of that I have no doubt.

But Mum is nothing if not relentless, and she would never allow me to rest on my laurels. Under her tutelage, I'm fluent in four languages and speak two of them natively. And yet—

"Why is it you still haven't started Spanish or German?" Mum would obtrude. "After all, they're related to languages you already speak, so they should be easy for you."

The fact that she's right doesn't necessarily make it any easier to accept. I suppose, in the end, it's just not easy living with the feeling you're always failing to live up to someone else's expectations. And when that someone started from nothing and, through sheer force of will, managed to become both highly successful and inordinately prosperous . . .

Well, especially when that someone's your mother.

More for her sake than for my own, I manage to exert myself, put on my coat, paste on a smile, and follow her out the door. "Seattle awaits me," I repeated, though with decidedly less enthusiasm.

With my own dancing career beginning to wind down, the thought of becoming a society wife—replete with women's clubs and golf and art openings and charity events— sounded, well . . . dreadfully dull, actually.

Conversely, the desire to start a family of my own was beginning to weigh on me—and the inescapable albatross of my approaching thirtieth had just signed a five-year lease in my psyche.

I was in just such a ponderous frame of mind when I pondered my way inside a bookshop. With Christmas nearly upon us, salespeople were everywhere, and shoppers were busily bustling about. I was actually thinking they would have a cafe, and when they didn't, I took to browsing the new fiction table, the best sellers, the Oprah's Book Club's books.

I wondered idly if Dr. Phil would be available for marriage counselling. We could build him an extension off the west wing to stay in—or, for that matter, he could just have the west wing.

I realised I was being overly dramatic. People get married

every day, after all. It was for the best, really—the marriage. Everyone said so. I just couldn't quite shake the feeling that I wasn't getting married so much as I was being acquired: *"The ballerina wife would go so lovely with the summer cottage and the convertible, don't you agree?"*

It was here, lamenting in the compact disc section (should one go with the Brahms or the Carmina Burana?) that, quite unexpectedly, I saw Sebastian. He was leaning casually against a bookshelf, legs crossed and arms folded, looking directly at me, just waiting for me to notice him.

"Hello, Stefanie."

"Ash—is that you!? My God! What are you doing here?"

How different he was. His smile was genuine, but his eyes remained somewhat aloof.

"I think that was my line," he said.

Hugging him was the only thing to do. I pounced on him, and he was for a moment taken aback, but soon he was hugging me back—picking me up and turning me around. He set me down and we had one of those odd silences where you don't know what to say before we both spoke at once and started laughing.

"Ah . . . I live here, Stefanie. Don't tell me you've been here for years and it's only now our paths cross." He grinned.

2
Sebastian Soulier

He was never handsome—certainly not in a classic way. But nor was he plain. He was, I suppose you could say, striking, if one bothered to look. Otherwise, he was just as likely to be lost among the crowd. In fact, it's entirely possible I oughtn't have noticed him at all those many years ago if he hadn't been . . .

Before . . .

"Someone's in my spot," I announced to no one in particular. It wasn't actually "my spot," and anyway, we didn't have reserved places at the barre. It was just garden-variety de facto laziness, comfort, and inertia that we all tended to congregate daily in the same locations.

The barre wrapped around the walls of the studio, and for the warm-up, portable barres were brought into the centre of the room.

"My spot," since nearly the day I arrived, had always been front position far left. Lars, the ballet's director, had actually placed me there on my first day, and it was to there I had always returned.

Sensing my displacement, Zoe (my dear Zóza) looked at me and smiled. She was in "her spot," leg up and head to knee, stretching on a centre barre. She gestured with her hand and I relocated myself to the available space across from her, and I didn't notice Sebastian again until the centre barres were removed and the floor work began.

His body was more athletic than classically proportioned, and he struggled a bit with the allegro, being unfamiliar with our routine. Lars's combinations tended toward complexity a bit much anyway, I always felt.

But when the time came for leaps and turns, he came into his element. Even Freddy, our resident tour de force trickster, took a breath at Ash's elevation.

In the end, though, it was his transformation that really struck me. From being, upon first impression, almost painfully shy and reclusive, when Sebastian stepped on stage, he was reborn as the complete embodiment of his character.

He could be charming and flirtatious, and make you laugh at his antics. He could make your heart flutter with romance, or pump adrenalin with his jealous rage—make you fall in love or fear for your life. But whatever character he was playing— one was simply compelled to watch him.

Mum once told me that when Nureyev walked on stage—it didn't matter if it was a crowd scene, or the middle of some-one's solo—when he walked on stage, one was drawn to him by his very presence.

Mum called it "magnetism." That's what painfully shy intro-verted Ash had: magnetism.

Adagio

3
The Mechanism

Now . . .

"Mum is here for a conference, and I suppose I'm tagging along. I can't believe you're here! Mum will just die!"

"Let me take the two of you to dinner. It would be my treat, unless you have plans, of course," Ash said.

"No, we would love to!" I said, but no sooner had the words escaped my lips than I, too late, thought the better of it. Suddenly I was all too aware of making loose ends. I wasn't at all sure I wanted to have the three of us together. Too many questions. Mum saying too much, which I may not be able to steer.

Just then it occurred to me that the engagement ring might have already spilt the beans. Casually, I brought my hands together, right over left and breathed a sigh of relief to find the ring was not presently on display.

"You're still dancing?" he asked.

"Oh please, let's not go there just yet." It was a presumably safe and natural topic, but after the ring incident, I wanted to slow down and think things through before I opened my mouth.

He smiled and nodded slowly, with reserved eyes and an impish grin.

"Okay," he said, "the ballet here is good. So are the dancers," he went on, "but it's all wasted on Balanchine."

Despite his love of movement, Ash despised abstract ballet; thus, his negative feelings for Balanchine. He would get lazy in rehearsals, despondent even.

"It's like a bunch of chords being played at random," Ash would complain. "Maybe they go together in some 'music theory' sort of way, but they don't tell a story. Would you want to see a play with abstract acting?"

Reasoning with Ash: the fact that Balanchine choreographed more than just abstract ballets, I found long ago, was a lost cause.

What was I doing? Wasn't I getting married? Yes, of course I was. And soon enough, I would come clean, and we would dine with Mum and talk of the old days, and future plans, of marriage and children—but not just yet. However, by convincing myself that I would do just that allowed me, in time, to regain my composure. Certainly, there is no harm in waiting a bit. After all, it would be bad form simply to talk about myself. And with that, I put it away.

4
Kyla's Trick

So instead we walked and browsed and laughed. He told me of his new endeavour, and the difficulties involved in starting a dance company of his own. I asked innumerable questions, ever directing (perhaps deflecting) the conversation away from my own life.

We strolled to the fish market and down to the pier. A leisurely walk through Belltown, finding a cafe for a coffee and croissant along the way.

While the air had grown crisp, the dusk stubbornly refused to submit to the encroaching darkness.

Pausing for a moment to look out over the Puget Sound, Ash shook out a cigarette.

"Still smoking?" I asked.

"I quit years ago, but trying to get this company going—the grants, the non-profit status, directing and still dancing myself—has, well, given me a lot of excuses."

"Can you still smoke in Seattle? I thought it was banned everywhere."

"Well," Ash said, "let's pretend it's a joint. That's legal. And besides, I'm feeling rebellious."

I smile, and in my best demure reply, *"C'est une belle nuit pour une rébellion* (It's a beautiful night for a rebellion), teasing him just a little.

Ash squinted his eyes and gave me a nescient glance. Despite his ancestry, Ash had never actually learned to speak French. I used to endlessly poke fun at him about it, but perhaps just now was still too soon. So instead I asked—

"Still smoking Nat Sherman's?"

"They're a quality smoke," Ash said, and then he started laughing.

"When I first met you, you still called them fags!"

"I haven't said that in years," I said, a little abashed.

"You remember that time you were out of cigs, so you asked Richie if he could 'spare a fag?' He knew what you meant, but offered up Enrico anyway. 'Bring him back in one piece, honey, he's the only one I have.'"

"I was still fresh off the boat," I laughed, slightly embar-rassed. I was actually a couple of years off the boat by then, but old habits wither slowly.

"At least I never fainted," I countered.

"Fainted!?"

"Must I remind you of the time you let Alexi take us all for drive in your mother's new Volvo?"

Ash squinted his eyes as he recalled the incident. Our Russian dancers had a predilection for European cars, and Alexi was no exception. He had unrelentingly pestered Ash to drive it until Ash finally caved.

"We drove too far and ended up being late to rehearsal. When Lars asked where we'd been, Alexi was so excited he exclaimed in broken English in front of the whole company, 'I'm so gratified! My boyfriend Ash just let me ride his mother's Vulva!'"

To be fair, Ash didn't actually faint, but held his head in his hands knowing he was going to be the butt of jokes for weeks to come.

Ash shook his head, laughing. "That has got to be the single most horrifying sentence ever uttered. Good for you, Stefanie. In less than an hour's time, you've been able to ruin literally years in therapy."

As memories of the two of us teasing one another came to mind, an almost tactile sensation began to arise within me: rekindled feelings both warm and familiar, and it hadn't taken long.

Ash took out his lighter, but with the wind gusting, actually lighting his cigarette was proving difficult.

"You need to use Kyla's trick," I said.

"What?"

"You remember Kyla—she danced with us back in the day?"

"Of course," replied Ash, though still uncertain where I was headed.

"Here," I said, taking his lighter and cigarette. I slid my hand with the lighter under my sweater, and with the cigarette held in my mouth, used the other hand to stretch the collar forward. This allowed enough room to drop the lighting end down below the fabric. Using the sweater as a shield, I was able to light the cigarette easily.

"Well, look at you," said Ash, impressed.

I draw in softly at first, then more deeply. As I close my eyes, the old familiar dizziness welcomes me, and with it, images from the past paint my imagination.

I exhale slowly out my nose and cough just a little at the end.

"See how well that works?" I say. "That's Kyla's trick."

Ash drew close and cocked his head to the side. Doing his best James Bond, he whispered, "I think you just wanted to put your lips on my butt."

"Nutter!" I laughed, then sputtered a bit more.

"Been a while?" Ash asked, smiling.

I looked at him then, taking him in. His smile, his hazel eyes—eyes I had once taken for granted but now had not seen in such a very long while. And without really being aware of it, colour had just returned to my world.

I inclined my head to the side and, still looking at him, relished a last drag before handing it back, "A while," I said.

5
Silences

After a time, our walk began to find its cadence. A topic would come up—a shared memory, perhaps—and we would happily chat away for a time until the subject exhausted itself. Then we would fall into silence, and those silences became more uncomfortable—yet at the same time, more enticing. Then another topic would appear, and we would be off chatting again.

It occurred to me that I ought to—out of politeness, if nothing else—ask if I was keeping him from something (or someone). But I was fearful of the answer—and anyway, I reasoned, in that way that I do, in that cacophony of stratagems I call my mind . . . my mechanism, he'd surely mention it if he was otherwise engaged.

Nutcracker season was ending (probably), and he was likely on break until the new year. And lastly, didn't he already say something about dinner? Obviously, he was free until then. And that should do it. No further inquiry required. And I let the matter drop for the moment to the back burner.

After visiting the Space Needle and the Chihuly Garden, we found ourselves in just such a silence. The sky, finally relenting, was beginning to darken, and the wind had started picking up.

"So . . ." Ash said, breaking the awkwardness. He placed his hands in his pockets and raised his shoulders against the wind, "have you given some thought to dinner? The Monorail is right here, and in two minutes it will whisk us back to where we started."

"A round trip then?" I laughed.

"Whatever you're in the mood for, really," he smiled warmly. "It's my treat. Should you call your Mom?"

And here it was, laid out before me. Suddenly, the high point in the dramatic line, the critical moment in my improvised play. It was a known build-up: a standard tension-getter. Nothing more than a soap opera device, really . . . Yet it was my soap, and the weight of it caught me unexpectedly.

It all hinges upon what she does next. The audience is transfixed. Tune in next week. No one in the theatre breathes.

"I think, probably . . . Mum is tired," I managed finally. "The flight and the conference."

Ash nods slowly, then turns and seems to look right through me. "I'm sure she wants no more than to curl up with a good book," he said. The wolf in his eyes, his hunger saying more.

'I'll go mad if this keeps up,' I anguish, as a perfect storm of desire and guilt begins buffeting about my insides — *'Mad as a hatter.'*

6
Tête-à-tête

"Why don't you come meet Jasper?" Ash said, breaking my spell. I took a breath and tried to relax a little.

"Jasper?" I inquired, curious.

"My apartment is near, and we can warm up," he said.

"Jasper's your son?" I asked—choosing for the moment to ignore the coincidental proximity of his said flat.

"I don't have a son. Jasper's my cat."

"Cat? I thought you were allergic."

"Well, I was, but one day I found him for adoption in a book-store and, well, we fell in love."

Ash owned a condo in lower Queen Anne. Full of character, it was a charming old "bricks and mortar." He said when he first bought it, one could walk outside and look up to the Space Needle. That was before a modern monstrosity of an apartment complex was erected just behind his building.

As the twilight faded to darkness, a light snow began to cover the ground while the wind gusted even more.

As Ash opened the door, an enormous fluffy cat approached and flopped on his back in that mysterious way that only cats know how to perform.

"Ash, he's enormous!"

"He's a Maine Coon—they're big kitties."

"Well hello, Mr. Jasper," I said, reaching down. Jasper sniffed my hand for a moment, then deciding I was friendly, allowed me to scratch his head.

While the building was constructed in the late thirties, the inside had been refurbished: light hardwood floors, and very open. A makeshift barre stood alongside the wall, on which was mounted a large mirror. Christmas lights wound around the ceiling, and a Christmas tree in the corner blinked its colours.

Ash clicked a button, and music began playing softly in the background. "Let me turn on some more light," he said.

"Wait," I said, a little too quickly. "I mean, I love Christmas lights, they're so pretty."

"Stefanie," he asked, opening a bottle of merlot and proceeding to pour us two glasses, "do you remember that piece we did? The in-house performance choreographed by that high school apprentice?"

"Yes," I laughed. "Danielle was her name, wasn't it? That was fantastic—but oh my god, so unsubtly sexual."

"I know," Ash replied, "I was a little embarrassed, or maybe embarrassed for her. But her choreography—so mature. I think that piece got her a scholarship to Banff."

"So . . ." Ash continued, returning to his original question, "what about you, Stefanie—are you still dancing? Are you and Zoe still the Dynamic Duo?"

At the mention of Zoe, my melancholy returned. Zóza had been away for over a year now, and I had been missing her terribly.

I mentioned to Ash that I was considering more and more the idea of retiring. But it occurred to me then that this consideration had begun only with Zóza's absence in my life. That, and meeting Marcus.

I had met Marcus not long before she left. He had wined and dined me, and for a while it had been a more than welcome distraction. But without Zoe's mellifluous presence in my life—along with the promise of "the good life" after dancing that Marcus offered—I began to entertain other choices, and other directions.

"Won't you miss dancing, Stefanie?" Ash asked seriously.

"I can't dance forever," I said.

"What do you mean?" Ash exclaimed. "Alisa Alonso performed into her seventies. Even your idol Sylvie Guillem danced till she was fifty! And anyway, fifty's still what—three or four years away?"

"You arse—take it back!" I protested, his teasing drawing me back to the present.

"Seriously, Stef, what else do you want to do? Become a trophy wife? Start a nuclear family? Find some rich patron to marry? A penthouse in New York, a villa in Spain, a bungalow in Barbados? Private jets and Sunday morning outings in the convertible?"

I felt my face flush at that—at the mention of the convertible—but said nothing.

"It's something to do, and I'm not judging," he continued. "I don't doubt it would be entertaining for a while, but would it . . .?"

Ash searched for the words.

"Look, you remember when Freddy and I were roommates?" he went on.

"Freddy? Of course I do!" I said, rolling my eyes. Freddy was not someone easily forgotten. "Are you still in touch?"

"We used to joke all the time about how, after a while, dancing was just like having a regular job. Well, once he left the company, he married a girl and went into tech."

"Freddy got married!?" I said, surprised.

"He went for the money and the stuff. And now? He's divorced and fresh out of rehab, trying to get back to art. What I'm saying is, Freddy thought dancing was just like having a regular job—until he got a regular job."

Ash continued, "He was never happy with corporate life. He said some people defined themselves by their work, but he never could because his heart wasn't in it. He got depressed and started to indulge in alcohol too much."

"I thought Freddy was gay?!"

"The point is," Ash said, ignoring me, "is that if you have a passion for something, and a huge talent and facility like you have, don't squander it."

"Freddy is straight?" I said, intentionally belabouring the point. "I wish I had known—he was super cute!"

"Stefanie!" Ash implored, "I'm being serious! This is your life."

I sighed a long exhalation before continuing, "I know," I relented, finally, "I'm sorry, Ash, I do think about it. I think about it all the time. Truth be told, it weighs heavy on me."

"I'm sorry, Stefanie," he said, sensing my change in demeanour. "I didn't mean to put you on the spot. I didn't know it was something you were . . . struggling with. Please, talk to me about your mom."

"Mum? I want to hear about Freddy!"

7
Freddy Danielsson

Lars Lavigne, the director of Capital City Ballet spotted Frederik Danielsson in a mass audition class and hired him as a soloist on the spot.

He was about five-seven or eight, impish and elf-like, technically adroit and possessed an amazing ballon. He brought such a light touch to his dancing. Whereas Sebastian's technique was powerful, Freddy's was nimble. He was able to land from large leaps with barely a sound.

Particularly suited to *A Midsummer Night's Dream* type of roles, he hailed from Norway where apparently his life partner Julian still lived.

Needless to say, Freddy was entertaining both on and off the stage.

Before . . .

"Gross!" Freddy yelled over his shoulder as he ambled across the studio, "not for five bucks!" When suddenly, as if struck by a revelation, Freddy froze. A mischievous grin slowly began to spread across his face.

"Alright, alright—I'll do it," he relented, springing back to life and suddenly changing his tune, "but Enrico—*you're* buying the drinks after the show!"

Freddy jogged towards the far corner of the studio where Zoe and I were stretching. "Hey," Freddy said quietly as he knelt down, "do one of you girls have some lotion?"

"Like, hand lotion?" I asked as Zoe dug around in her bag.

"Yeah, hand lotion, suntan lotion, whatever." Freddy grinned as Zoe handed him a few travel-sized bottles.

"You can just have it," she said, "I stocked up at the hotel in Vancouver."

"Perfect!" he said.

Freddy rose, slipped the bottles into the pocket of his hoodie, and started to walk away. Then he paused and turned back to us. With a quintessential "Freddy-esque" mixture of perplexity and amusement adorning his face he asked, "Well, are you girls coming or not!?"

Zoe and I looked at each other and roused ourselves off the floor.

Freddy, a good-natured but irrepressible prankster, had something in mind. While we didn't know what he was up to—and certainly not wanting to encourage such behaviour— we weren't about to miss it either.

Ash had just walked into the studio when Freddy stopped

him. Ash listened, pursed his lips, and nodded, then turned and followed Freddy back to the lobby.

Unless we had actual guests or an in-house performance, the lobby served as more of a dancers' lounge when not rehearsing.

Sebastian was leaning against the window separating the lobby and the studio. He spotted us and waved us over.

"What's Freddy up to?" I asked.

"He didn't say," Ash said. "Only something about needing protection, and he asked me to run interference, so god only knows."

Freddy walked over to where Enrico was sitting on the edge of a sofa.

"Sorry, Freddy," explained Enrico, "Richie said he'd do it, but he kept putting it off. Last year I had it waxed, but it's too late to schedule an appointment, and anyway, that shit hurts! And I'd still be all red tonight. I just don't want to go on stage looking like a dancing bear."

Enrico Romano was performing Arabian in this year's *Nutcracker*. As the piece is generally performed shirtless, he needed some assistance removing some excess body hair.

Enrico, while a real sweetheart was, shall we say . . . well suited to cold climates. Specifically, he was asking for someone to apply hair removal cream to his back. And as dire need and exceptionally poor judgement would have it . . . that someone turned out to be Freddy.

"No worries mate," said Freddy, all the while doing his best to keep a straight face. "Turn around."

As Freddy prepared, he kept smirking in our direction.

With Enrico's shirt off and facing away, Freddy applied the hair removal cream to his back, sticking out his tongue and making disgusted faces to us as he did so.

"What do you think, leave it on about five minutes?" asked Enrico.

"I'd give it a solid hour," joked Freddy. "I found a nest of baby mice back there. They're marching their burnt hairless backsides down to the SPCA as we speak."

As he spoke, Freddy quickly removed the application glove he was wearing and emptied three bottles of Zoe's lotion into the palm of his hand.

"Oh, Freddy . . ." whispered Zoe, shaking her head.

Freddy lifted his heavily lotioned palm above Enrico's head. With his other hand, he raised a finger and giving us one last look of unbridled amusement, let the suspense build.

"Oh fuck!" said Ash, bringing his hand to his forehead, finally understanding.

Freddy slapped his lotion-filled palm down en masse on top of Enrico's head and began to rub it furiously in his hair.

Enrico straightened immediately, his body stiff with tension. Thinking he was going to end up with a monk's spot in his precious mane, Enrico bounded off the sofa.

"Motherfucker!" he yelled, as he started chasing a chortling Freddy around the lounge.

Freddy leaped over the sofa, over chairs, and over other dancers while Enrico, knocking anything in his path, his back still white with cream and head dripping with lotion, charged after him like a Pamplona bull pissed on red.

When Freddy ducked back into the studio, Ash blocked the door and had to physically restrain Enrico from charging through.

"Hold on there, big guy," said Ash, bracing himself in the door frame. As Zoe and I ran over to help, we picked up the empty bottles along the way to show him it was harmless.

With Ash's assistance, and multiple assurances from Zoe and me that it was just regular lotion, Enrico eventually cooled off and Freddy avoided an inevitable beating. Though, had Enrico actually caught him, Freddy probably would have just died laughing.

* * *

"Dammit, Freddy!"

Jesminder Patel had been in the middle of rehearsal when she suddenly stopped what she was doing and began to look intently in the mirror.

Freddy's latest masterpiece involved applying moisture-activated ink to Jess's leotard which, thirty minutes into rehearsal, resulted in two one-eyed smiley faces slowly emerging over her breasts.

"Why don't you grow up?" Jesminder hissed as she stormed out the studio to go change.

Suppressed laughter followed Jess, for as she turned, she revealed two handprints on her arse, the words 'Fresh Mango' written on her lower back, followed by a downward arrow.

* * *

There was a general consensus among the company that Vincent Wolfe's hygienic acumen *lacked profundity.*

After a number of friendly mentions, Freddy grew tired of Vinnie's smelly unwashed tights stinking up the men's locker room day in and day out and decided the time had come to take more decisive action.

He proceeded to soak Vinnie's dance belt in an extra-strength Tiger Balm solution, topping it off with a few shots of pepper spray he had borrowed from one of the girls. He allowed it to thoroughly dry, ensuring Vinnie wouldn't feel any warmth until activated by perspiration.

Vinnie, who was performing the pas de deux from *Don Quixote* that evening, managed the opening without distress. It wasn't until coming offstage at the end of the male variation that the discomfort really began.

As he watched Clair perform her variation from the wings, Vincent began shifting from foot to foot, started to squirm, and then began prancing about in place.

"Is everything alright, Vinnie?" asked a well-pleased Freddy. "You look like you've got some mites in your tights."

Vince gave Freddy a suspicious glare, but with Clair just finishing her solo, had to go back on stage.

Vinnie, who famously danced slightly behind the beat, was now starting to rush everything and was rhythmically all over the place.

While dancers started gathering in the wings to watch the amusements, true hilarity only ensued during the final poses, usually snapshot moments of no movement.

Profusely sweating from his forehead, Vinnie supported Clair's waist for her final pirouettes, ending in a *croise derriere* attitude pose.

In perfect balletic symmetry, Clair faced the audience and held her pose. Her left leg supporting her beneath, her right wrapped in attitude around Vinnie's torso.

While standing directly behind her, his hands on Clair's waist, Vinnie's burning groin caused his hips to grind and undulate in a suggestive and not very balletic fashion.

At this point, Lars, who had guessed something was awry, began gesturing wildly with his hands for us to back away from the wings as our laughter was becoming both audible and contagious to the audience.

Ash referred to Vincent as a "Curtain Call Cowboy": That is, a performer who insisted the curtain rise again and again, compelling the audience to continue clapping—milking the applause—well past its natural conclusion.

This time, however, Vinnie managed exactly one grimaced

bow before rushing to the wings, leaving Clair alone on stage when the curtain rose for the remainder of the adulations.

Vince sprinted to his dressing room only to find Freddy had placed there a single red rose stuck in the middle of a bucket of ice, a new dance belt, and a card with the words *"Just Say No to Crotch Rot"* written on the inside.

Other prankster miscellany included, but was not limited to, switching the quick-change performance tights of Richard Bachman (6'3") with those of Camila Rodriguez (4'11").

His "prank de résistance," however, was still a good year away from being discovered.

8
Incident at Hamburger Mary's

At the same time, Freddy could be fiercely protective of those he cared about—to the point of foolishness based on his stature. This tendency toward protectiveness was compounded with the consumption of alcohol. And despite his small stature, Freddy could and would drink everyone under the table.

One evening after the day's rehearsals, Freddy, Zoe, and I were at Hamburger Mary's having a drink and waiting for our food.

In a window booth at the other end of the bar, a team of college jocks were drinking and making a ruckus. A couple of them kept glancing over in our direction.

"I think you have some admirers," said Freddy.

Unfortunately, as it turned out, but naturally enough, Zoe and I, just for a moment, turned to see who it was before turning back around. This was apparently interpreted as flirting, and after a few minutes—once their alcoholic thirst was satiated, and requisite brash courage summoned—a couple of them invited themselves to our table.

They began friendly enough.

"My friend and I was wonderin ifin y'all'd like to dance?" one of them said.

He stood about six foot five and at least 250 pounds. His sleeves were rolled up to his elbows and large veins were protruding from his forearms. Despite his size, however, he was dwarfed by the immensity of his friend who, so far, had only stared.

"Why thank you," said Freddy, giving them a dreamy look. "I'd be enchanted."

"We was asking the ladies," the big one chimed in.

Freddy just shrugged his shoulders and returned to his drink.

"I'm sorry," I said. "We've been rehearsing all day—"

"And I'm afraid we're all danced out," finished Zoe. "Need to rest our weary bones."

"If y'all are sore, I'm sure we could work out some of your kinks for ya," said the bigger one. As he spoke, he kneaded his enormous hands in the air, perhaps hoping a visual aid would enhance his "seduction"; as the reek of their inebriation wafted over to us, it certainly needed something.

"That's a kind offer," I said, "but I'm afraid we have a physical therapist already."

"He's the only one allowed to work on us, for insurance reasons," Zoe added.

"Hear that, Johnny?" the little one laughed. "Insurance reasons."

"Y'all look like dancers," said Johnny, "I mean, Jimmy and me, we's just wantin' to show our appreciation. Seems to me it idn't right ifin y'all ain't gonna be friendly."

Angered by our rejection, Jimmy became nastier, "Do they like, take out a policy on your whole body?" he asked, amused by his own "so-called" wit, "or are some parts worth more than others? Hey, Johnny, which part would you like a policy on? I sure the fuck know what parts I'd insure."

I was starting to become uncomfortable, and sensing this, Zoe placed her hand on my own.

"Oh looky here!" Jimmy said, pointing to our hands. "Did you see that, Johnny? I'd sure like to pack some meat into that lesbo sandwich."

I could see the tension in Freddy's face winding up, and I had a feeling that if I didn't do something soon, it was only going to get worse.

"Listen—" I started.

"We're sorry," said Zoe, "but we really have had a long day—"

"And we just want to finish our drinks in peace," I finished.

Freddy, who at this point had had quite enough, turned to face them.

Veins of his own were now visible on his forehead. With a forced calmness he said, "Listen, Jimmy-Bob and—Little John, was it?—the ladies said they weren't interested."

The two of them turned to face Freddy. Together, they

undoubtedly outweighed Freddy by at least four hundred pounds. The look on their collective faces seemed to regard him about as consequential as an oil stain on a garage floor.

"We talking to the ladies, Matchbox," said Little John, "and I don't think ladies is exactly your thang. So why you wanna go play hero, son? There a boy here you tryin' to impress? He as small as you? Hell, maybe we'll call him Thimble. Matchbox and the Thimble: sort of a Thelma and Louise for the anally inclined."

Seeing the look of Freddy's face, a surge of adrenaline kicked my pulse up another notch.

Mike the bartender had been taking notice of the situation and asked, "Everything alright over there?"

Jimmy turned and held up his hand. "We good, we good, we just gettin' to know one another," then, turning back to us, quietly he said, "nice and intimate-like."

With marked restraint, Freddy said, "come on girls, let's go," then to Mike, "Would you put this on my tab? I'll come back to pay for it later."

When Freddy stood up, "Little John" towered at least a foot over him.

"Goddamn, Johnny!" chuckled Jimmy, "you-is-ah good notch taller than the Matchbox here."

Freddy just stared at him. "Not your notch," he said.

Jimmy chuckled, "Not my notch, that's a good one," and then he lurched at Freddy, feinting an attack. But Freddy didn't flinch.

Mike, appalled at having his regular customers treated rudely, yelled to the kitchen staff for backup.

"I think it's time for you to leave," Mike said, walking towards our table.

"What'ed you say?" asked Little John as he lifted a hand the size of a catcher's mitt to Mike's chest. "Sorry, but I don't speak faggot." With a flick of his wrist, Mike rebounded off his hand and stumbled back several steps to the bar.

"Come on now, y'all ain't gonna leave, not without a dance," Jimmy said, "if you ain't up to a slow dance, you could just hop up on the table here and give us a show."

Zoe and I were up off our stools, but with the "corps de jock" blocking our exit, we were left standing alongside the table.

"Or we could just sit back down, and you could entertain us properly," added Little John, as he scooped a huge wad of chewing tobacco into his mouth.

"After all, we's paying customers. Y'all a couple of pros— that's what pros do right?—Dance for money? Hell—I got a five on me right now," said Little John as he pulled some bills from his pocket. Dropping his voice to a whispered growl, he continued, "Honey, y'all just show me where you want me to stick it."

I grabbed Zoe's hand and tried to slide through anyway, when Jimmy stepped directly in front of us.

"Now wait a minute," he said. "We ain't finished negotiating. How much y'all charge to take a lick at my policy?" he said, grabbing his crotch, "I'm thinkin' you spending so much time with butt pirates and sodomites you've forgotten what a real man feels like."

Then, with the same hand Jimmy used to grab his crotch, he reached up and stroked my face.

And seeing that, Freddy broke.

With legs firing like pistons, Freddy exploded into the air—leaping so high he simultaneously grabbed the back of Little John's head and yanked it down full force to meet his upcoming right knee, striking him squarely in the face.

Jimmy seemed to watch in slow motion as Little John toppled over backward, the back of his head hitting the bar's foot rail on the way down, knocking him out cold. Blood from his mouth spilled out and began to pool across the floor.

A stunned Jimmy turned back only to find Zoe, quick as a cat, knee cocked to her chest and leg sprung like a scorpion's tail, thrusting her Pavlovian-pointed foot full force deep into his solar plexus.

Jimmy folded in half over the power of Zoe's thrust until, knocked squarely off his balance point, he ended up on the ground alongside his friend, holding his abdomen and gasping.

The rest of the jocks were now up and advancing in our direction but came full stop at a shotgun Mike had pulled from behind the bar. "I said, it's time for you to leave!" he yelled. A double barrel pointed squarely in their direction. "Now pick up your sorry ass friends and get the hell out of my place!"

We were hurriedly on our way out the door as in walked a smiling Sebastian. "Where you guys going!?" Ash said. "I just got—"

He looked past us and surveyed the fallout in "Hamburger Armageddon": stools knocked over, two huge men on the ground, blood pooling across the floor, and Mike the friendly bartender pointing a shotgun at an angry mob. "What the *fuck* happened here!?" Ash exclaimed.

Taking Zoe by the hand and passing him on the way out, Freddy replied, "Never fuck with a ballet dancer who has PTSD."

"Come on, Sebastian," I said, grabbing his arm and leading him away down the street.

Years later, Mum adopted a Jack Russell Terrier. A small dog, but absolutely *fearless*. Recalling my tale from Hamburger Mary's and much to my utter dismay, Mum named him Freddy.

9
Prank de Résistance

Now . . .

"So, Freddy married . . . a girl? Did he want to have children?" I asked.

Ash dropped his head to his hands and laughed, "Well, Stef, I'm not sure how to begin—"

"Did Fiona try and turn him?" I interrupted. "She always was such a fag-hag."

This brought on a fresh wave of laughter. Ash was sputtering so much from it his eyes were tearing. "Ahh, how does one say it?" Ash said, trying to compose himself and failing. "Let's just say . . . Freddy may not have been quite as gay as we thought!"

"What?"

"Fiona may have tried to turn him—but by the time she had Freddy in her sights, he'd probably slept with half of the girls in the company!"

"What!?" I repeated, staring dumbfounded.

41

"Throw a spanner in your works?" said Ash, playfully mocking my accent.

"Who!?" I implored.

"I'm not going to name names."

"Mime it!" I demanded. And not remotely dissuaded, I continued, "Okay, Fiona, who else—Mira?"

Ash said nothing, but his eyes rolled up.

"Clair?"

He ran a hand over his scruff.

"I must have been completely oblivious," I said.

"You all were at the time. I was his roommate, so I had a bit more knowledge of his comings and goings. You have to admit it was a brilliant ruse."

"What do you mean?"

"Girls love gay men. They treat them like one of 'the girls,' so to speak. Eventually, at some point, the discussion turns to sex, and 'Did he always know he was gay?' and 'Has he ever been with a woman?' Perhaps he says no, but—he has always been curious—and I'm assuming you can guess the rest."

"Are you guessing, or did you know?" I inquired, sensing an accomplice.

"He made amends with me recently as part of his program, and as rigorous honesty is a part of it. He admitted as much."

"But at the time I didn't ask, and he didn't say. I had a good sense of what was happening. I suspected, but honestly, I didn't want to be put in a position of knowing."

"Meaning?"

"I extrapolated. Being his roommate, seeing him unguarded—his 'lover,' to whom he was supposedly ever-faithful off in a distant country, keeping him from forming much in the way of relationships with gay men in the company."

"'Extrapolated!?' My, someone's been improving their vocabulary," I teased.

"Look, Freddy sensed an opportunity," he went on, "and anyway, to be honest, I'm not sure how the Bro Code applies here."

"Bro Code?"

"Yeah, I mean, he never did anything illegal, nor did he make any promises. Morally ambiguous to be sure, but . . ." Ash shrugged his shoulders. "You have to admit, it was rather well done."

"What is a Bro Code?"

"Google it."

"Why didn't he ever approach me?" I asked after a moment—unsure if I was relieved or insulted.

"When I saw him, his confession was so heartfelt, I didn't think to ask. So—and I'm guessing here—but he knew you and I were close, and I imagine he knew I'd be more than displeased if he did something dishonest involving you."

"Displeased?" I taunted.

"That's the word I used."

"Why, how 'Mr. Darcy' of you!" I teased. "Please continue, oh guardian of women's honour!"

Sebastian laughed and blushed slightly.

"Well, apparently he was eventually outed—or perhaps in this case, "inned." But by that time, we had both left the company. I came up here, and I think you and Zoe had left for Texas by then."

Rigorous honesty? I thought to myself. *Lord that must be exhausting . . . or would it be quite possibly a relief?*

"What about Zoe? Did she ever say anything?" Ash asked.

"If she was ever with Freddy, she didn't mention it," I said doubtfully, "and Zoe and Freddy were partnered together as often as we were."

"By the way," I continued, changing the subject as one old memory led to another, "do you remember the pool party? All the straight men were disappointed when Zoe came out with a one-piece on instead of a bikini."

"We weren't *that* disappointed," Ash said, smiling. I could tell he was reminiscing.

"Actually," he went on, "that was my first inkling that Freddy may not be on the up and up in the orientation department. I remember all the gay men were hooting and hollering when she came out like it was a drag show— *'You go girl!'* and all that. The straight men were more, shall we say, focused. And Freddy was quietly observing. I'll never forget that look. He was hardly over the top, but in that moment, he looked distinctly un-gay."

"I remember you two having turning contests all the time," I said, referring to Zoe.

"We had a very different style."

"And her winning," I teased.

"Did you hear the part about us having a different style?"

"I guess her style was to turn effortlessly and end up balanced in attitude, and yours was to fall flat on your arse?"

Ash squinted. "That happened one time . . . *I can't believe you remember that!"*

10
Zoe Bryne

Before . . .

With platinum-blond hair, cut in a Miss Fisher twenties bob that just suited her, Zoe—aka, "the Beast," aka, "the Bell"— Bryne was an audacious, devil-may-care, free-spirited import from Australia. She was funny, vivacious, game for a laugh, and forever, interminably, late to rehearsal.

She also, for a ballerina, possessed certain physical attributes not typically associated with female dancers.

She was forever forgetting her keys, or her phone, or her bag. So much so that Freddy, again the prankster, once went to the trouble of buying her an enormous mason jar and placing it on the counter of the ballet's reception area where the rest of the company could deposit her various items found scattered about the studios.

Her own personal lost and found, as it were.

Titling it "The Bell's Jar," Freddy intended it as a bit of a joke—a somewhat macabre reference to Sylvia Plath—but, being Zoe, she actually was rather touched by the gesture.

An elite turner, she would do a slow three or four full inward attitude turns then gradually straighten up and bring her arms in, keeping the speed consistent, for another four or five— then pop back into attitude and balance there for days.

This ability, alongside her effortlessly languid ballet technique, earned her the nickname "the Beast."

She was kind, generous, nurturing, and extremely well liked—in spite of her foibles. And she had something else . . .

Zoe possessed an eidetic memory: *She had only to see her parts once.*

This ability was not only limited to her own parts. Zoe could remember everyone's part, in every ballet she had ever taken part in, since the time she was eleven or twelve.

When she watched choreography, she became completely absorbed. She told me once that when she watches dance, the outside world becomes very quiet.

This gift extended beyond choreography.

Once at a party, a couple of wine coolers in her, she casually corrected her date on his recollection of a Tyson fight while he was speaking with his mates. The question was, of which round a knockout occurred in.

The YouTube oracle was consulted, and sure enough, she was right.

If that weren't enough, she then proceeded to mime Tyson's entire round from memory, as Tyson, in time, in front of the TV for comparison.

It was an uncanny demonstration to say the least, and more than a little bit eerie—at least, so thought her date, who apparently felt her freak factor outweighed her physical attributes.

Zoe was at a loss as to why her relationship suddenly ended. After all, they were having such a good time. However, in possession of a jubilant personality and never in want of men, her despondency was short-lived.

When she wasn't rehearsing or otherwise engaged, she was reading fantasy literature. And when she was reading, like dance, she was completely absorbed.

She once mentioned that while reading in her flat, the building's fire alarm was triggered. Luckily, it was a false alarm, as she didn't even hear it. A bit embarrassed, she only found out about it the following day when speaking with neighbours.

Her memory extended to her reading as well. While I never asked her to read verbatim passages from memory, she would often paraphrase the action taking place on any page of her book.

To this day, Zoe remains my best friend and confidant. I love Zóza like the little sister I never had.

11

From "Beast" to "Bell"

Zoe, when not rehearsing herself, typically watched the "goings-on" in her "Planet Zoe" fashion. Absorbing everything, until the choreography was set. Following that, if she wasn't chatting away with someone, she plopped herself down and read.

Her absorption was so complete, however, that when again needed for rehearsal, she couldn't be roused from her book by calling her name—despite being less than twenty feet from the action.

Lars had to have someone go physically rouse her, and even this wasn't an easy task. A hand on her shoulder wouldn't do it. Nor would a gentle shake.

"Okay, whose turn is it to rouse the Beast?" Lars would ask. "Freddy, would you mind going and tipping over Zoe again?"

"She's already laying down," Freddy laughed. Obviously, this only worked when she was sitting up.

"Kyla," Lars continued, "would you be so kind as to help Freddy grab a foot and drag the Beast back to rehearsal?"

Kyla took a moment and curtsied first to Lars, then the rest of the company before chasséing "Ky-esque-ly" over to help Freddy demonstrate to the company the proper care and etiquette required when Beast-dragging.

Each grabbing a pointe-shoed foot, Freddy and Kyla gently dragged Zoe halfway to the centre of the studio, before her spell was broken.

While undoubtedly amusing, in time, this trait became such a nuisance that eventually Lars took Zoe aside.

"He was very sweet," she told me later. "He said I wasn't in any trouble, but that my 'Beast Sleep' as he called it, was wasting time, making me late for rehearsals, and causing rehearsals to go long. He asked me if there was anything that could be done."

Zoe sat and quietly listened, her large brown doe eyes taking it all in until Lars finished what he had to say. She then opened her purse, dug for a moment, and produced a small bell.

Handing it to Lars, she said, "this is what my parents used — they made me bring it with me." Then she got up and walked to the door. Pausing momentarily, she glanced back. "I guess my brain is just sort of tuned to it."

When I imagine what must have been *the look of bewilderment* on Lars's face, a lifetime supporter of women's rights, when Zóza handed him that bell — the whole Pavlovian response notion running through his mind — I just have to laugh.

"Good Lord" he thought, shaking his head. *If the papers got a hold of this . . .*

Later, Lars confessed to me, he was concerned that a story would break reporting that a male director was ringing a bell to summon scantily clad females to do his bidding. It was more than he was willing to chance. So, for the time being he continued to tolerate Zoe's beast sleeps.

He ended up placing the bell on a shelf in the back of a lecture podium alongside rosin and elastic, some old pointe shoes someone had left, needles and thread for quick shoe emergencies, and his morning coffee.

One morning during rehearsals late the following week, while reaching for his coffee, Lars accidentally knocked the bell off the ledge. When it hit the floor, Zoe—who at that point had been stretched out in usual fashion facing the corner on her tummy reading—immediately looked up from her book and glanced back over her shoulder.

After a moment of awed silence, Lars said, "Sorry, Zoe—false alarm. Please—as you were."

Zóza just smiled sweetly and returned to her book.

The rest of the dancers, both surprised and more than a little amused, looked back and forth a couple of times between Lars and Zoe. Then Freddy, unable to contain himself further, burst out laughing. This caused a general uproar in the studio, lasting the better part of fifteen minutes.

Zoe wouldn't have minded, but as it happened, with her book again in front of her, she didn't hear it. Thus, her sobriquet Zoe "the Bell" was born.

12
Altercations

Now . . .

"Ash, do you recall the night we performed for that corporate party? It was for 'Kit'n Whiskers,' wasn't it? Who'd have thought there was so much money in pet food!"

Ash shook his head. "I remember you gave me a roundhouse punch to the face I won't soon forget! Good lord, I did not see that coming!"

"I had to get you back for being such a bully in rehearsals."

It was a postseason performance. Much of the company gladly partook in the event as it provided a little extra cash for the lean summer months between seasons.

Ash and I were performing last: a pas de deux from Johan Sundström's *Tango*. Johan had flown in from New York to set it on us personally. Now that the choreography had been effectively blocked, Johan had flown home, and it was up to Ash and me to breathe some life into the piece.

The choreography begins with the woman walking away from

the man—spitefully ignoring him. He grabs her arm and spins her around to face him, at which point she slaps him across the face, and the dance begins . . .

Before . . .

"You're anticipating Stefanie," Ash critiqued.

"What?" I asked, slightly annoyed. After all, we were still in the intro—we hadn't even gotten to the actual "dancing" yet.

"You're slowing down as you walk past me—anticipating the arm grab and the spin. *Stop, doing that!* Listen, if I don't grab your arm, you should just walk offstage."

What I had been doing, of course, *was anticipating*. Slowing down and even lifting my arm slightly to facilitate his grab. It was choreography, after all—movements rehearsed and performed. Frankly, I didn't see the issue at first—even once I understood what he was talking about.

I took a breath and reminded myself not to take his criticism personally. It's a collaboration, after all.

"Look, Stefanie," he said, "anticipating may be okay if you're playing Giselle—*maybe*—but this piece is set in a fiery underground establishment in Argentina. It's dark, smoky—full of machismo and passion."

And yet, on he drones.

"We need to make this real, Stefanie. Stop being a 'dancer.' Instead, you need to be an actor through the vehicle of dance."

And on . . .

"Sanford Meisner called it, 'being real under imaginary circumstances,'" Ash continued. "This is the beginning of the piece, Stefanie. This moment sets the whole tone between us."

If the smouldering pit of ire gnawing at my belly was any indication, I was beginning to feel lectured to.

"You've heard the phrase 'the wilful suspension of disbelief?' It's what allows you to see a film or a ballet and let yourself get caught up in the story even though on some level you know it isn't real."

With my temper-ometer now blatantly flashing yellow, I was beginning to wonder exactly who had died and made Ash Ballet Master?

"I have heard of it" I snapped back. *"It's in iambic pentameter, isn't it?"*

"Whatever," he said.

That the beat was a little off, lessening my rebuke, further grated my nerves and I tossed the words about in my mind looking for a solution: "Su-<u>spen</u>-sion <u>of</u> my <u>wil</u>-ful <u>dis</u>-be-<u>lief</u>" would do it . . .

Focus, Stefanie! I reprimanded myself.

Frustration was causing my mind to spin off on a tangent— The point *was* I was simply letting Ash know he didn't have to "carte blanche" condescend to me—that he wasn't the sole purveyor of intelligence in the room.

Ash was so adamant about it that we worked on the opening over and over ad infinitum—nearly more than the rest of the piece altogether.

It should be so simple—yet it was so different from what I was used to that I was having difficulties getting it. And as I continued to struggle, my irritation became nearly tangible.

"No, Stefanie!" Ash groaned. *"Let's try it again."*

The more we rehearsed it, the more I failed, and the more I failed, the more churlish I became. Ash was aware of my increasing ill humour, but losing patience himself, he did not relent.

"Damn it, Stefanie!" He was clearly frustrated now, and on the verge of yelling. "Stop thinking about the choreography! Your only intention is getting the hell away from me. Really, it's not *that* difficult—*just walk off the goddamned stage!"*

Unable to contain my rancour, I went into full prima donna mode.

"Godverdomme Sebastian! Piss off, you bloody wanker!"

I grabbed my things, swung my dance bag over my shoulder, and stormed out.

"Stefanie . . . wait!" His tone was softer now, apologetic—but it was much too late.

"Krijg de Tering!" (Get Cancer!) I hissed, flicking a "V" in his face and knocking him with my shoulder as I passed.

Sebastian grabbed me by the arm and brazenly spun me

around—the force of which, sent my dance bag flying off my shoulder.

I was so shocked, and so livid, that I just stood there fuming—hexing him with diva venom seething from my eyes.

Ash's face lit up. *"That's it!—Oh my god, Stefanie, that's fucking perfect!*—Dance with me right now!"

I stood adamant, but his abrupt change of mood left me feeling confused.

"Please, Stef," Ash implored. "Come on, don't think— just move!"

Slowly I relented, but still rife with anger, fought his lead.

"Yes, that's it! You're not going to let a man tame you. This is a fight, not a fucking waltz! Bring it, bitch!"

In that moment, our dancing took on an entirely different character. With subtlety and nuance, our phrasing played with the rhythm of the music and little improvisations occurred within the choreography, never twice repeated.

I would fight his lead at different times, forcing him to compensate on the spot. At the same time, I threw myself into lifts and turns with abandon, trusting him to be there for me. Spurring him on in this manner my body felt a freedom I hitherto wasn't even aware was absent.

"Look at me, Stef!" Ash commanded. "Don't even think of turning away."

His gaze was immense. As I met his stare, in my peripheral

vision the studio seemed to fade, and in its place, it grew smoky, noisy, and dark.

I began to sense apparitions about the room. A bar complete with patrons now stood in front of the mirror, other shadow characters scattering out of our way as we danced.

A phantom chair we knocked to its side skidded across the floor. Music was no longer coming from the speakers but from spectre musicians playing in the smoky darkness.

This was not like anything I had previously envisioned, but it seemed to be happening spontaneously. It was the oddest, most exhilarating sensation I have ever felt. It was as if the dance, my body, and my imagination were dancing themselves, and I was simply along for the ride.

We finished exhausted, panting and drenched with sweat. With his hands on his knees, Ash and I glared at each other as we caught our breath. After a moment he approached me, and lifting my hand, kissed it.

Still breathing hard, he placed his hands on either side of my face, and holding my head in his hands, looked directly at me.

"Brilliant. You're fucking brilliant, Stefanie."

He kissed me softly on the forehead, met my eyes for a moment longer, and then touched my cheek with his hand.

"Thank you," he said. Then he turned around and walked out of the studio.

I stood dazed. My eyes were beginning to moisten, and my entire body tingled with aliveness. Other dancers had gathered to watch. They were looking at me, not warming up or chatting amongst themselves.

"Stefanie?" I looked up to see a concerned Zoe standing before me. Taking my hand, she picked up my bag and led me out.

"Come with me, Stevie, I'm taking you home."

As I walked out the studio, I seemed to exist outside myself.

It gave me so much insight into why Ash's stage presence was so magnetic. For him—it was real. My god, it made such a difference.

13
Tit for Tat

The slap, however, was an entirely different story. In rehearsals the next day, Ash implored me to really slap him rather than "mime it"— that is, missing his face altogether while he slapped his leg for a sound effect.

He said he had done something similar playing Don Jose in Thomas Hargrove's production of *Carmen* years before.

"Listen," he pleaded, "you really slap me, and I'll turn my head as you make contact. It will deflect the sting a bit and still make a decent sound—and besides, Stefanie, it gives such an air of authenticity to the performance."

Needless to say, I resisted. I made it clear I had no intention of slapping someone on stage for real. The grab was one thing, but the slap quite another.

As the show drew near and I continued to refuse, Ash, content with the grab and more than pleased with how the rest of the dance was coming, reluctantly resorted to slapping his leg.

All the while, in secret, I calculated my retribution.

14
Frappé en Face

We were nervous before the performance. The floor was not the marley flooring that we were used to, but some parquet dance floor they use at weddings, and it was—a dancer's worst nightmare—slippery as ice.

The music began, and as choreographed, I stormed past him.

And this time, when Ash grabbed my arm and spun me around, I did intend to surprise him with a good-natured slap.

But with our adrenaline pumping, Sebastian's grab was more forceful than usual. The slipperiness of the floor gave no resistance, and my spin was much faster than expected.

My arm lifted with the centrifugal force to help balance myself, but rather than spinning to a stop first and then slapping him with my fingers, with the momentum's extra force, the blow had the entire weight of the spin behind it. And it wasn't just my fingers, but the whole of my wrist that made contact with the side of his head.

I didn't slap Ash so much as clobbered him. I literally

stopped myself from spinning by hitting him in the head. Entirely unprepared for the blow, Ash was completely stunned—then he slowly turned back to me as his eyes caught fire.

Looking directly into his eyes, and meeting his intensity with my own, I whispered, "Ash—that was fucking perfect," and the dance proper began.

Needless to say, *we danced the fuck out of the thing that night.*

15
Entanglements

After the performance, we were expected to mingle among the guests, but it was near impossible to separate us. Always needing some form of physical contact—be it his arm around me or just our little fingers holding—my body yearned for the pleasant ache of his presence beside me.

Then James arrived. Late for the performance, he was nevertheless kind and a gentleman and—at the moment, at least—completely banal.

I had recently started seeing him. He was a corporate type, a lawyer, and his company had some sort of interest in CCB. We had met after a theatre performance earlier in the year. He had no real knowledge of ballet, and really no clue what-soever about artistic types. But he was sweet and attentive, if rather pedestrian.

He sensed no threat from Ash—he assumed all male dancers were poofs. I spotted him from across the room, and he held up his arm in a wave and began to approach.

I turned to face Ash, our hands at each other's elbows

and looked forlorn. Ash looked me in the eyes then, a little too long.

"What is it?" I asked.

For a few moments, Ash said nothing, but just continued to look at me—searching me with his eyes. Then he just managed a smile and kissed me on the cheek.

"Go on, Stefanie," he said quietly. "Your date awaits you."

Our hands continued to cling to one another as reluctantly I began to walk away, our arms rising slowly as we separated. My elation diminished as the distance increased, until it was impossible to hold on. First the one hand let go, and with another step, the other. As our remaining hand fell, so did my mood.

James met me with a hug and cheek kiss, and I managed a grimaced smile. I complained about the slipperiness of the floor, and how exhausted I was, downplaying the performance.

"Well, everyone I talked to said you were on fire tonight," he said.

I made it clear that It had been an exhausting week, and now, lying, said that my stomach was cramping. He seemed to take the hint and, after a bit more mingling, offered me a ride back to my flat.

* * *

"Thank you," I said as he dropped me off. "You really are very sweet," and meant it.

I kissed him quickly on the cheek and went inside. He waited for my wave from the window before driving off. As I watched him pull away, I was already dialling a taxi to transport me as quickly as possible back to the party.

In my scheming, I assumed James would not return to the party, but planned on keeping an eye out, nevertheless. If I did happen to run into him, I'd say I had forgotten my . . . what—costume?

"Don't you have costumers for that?" I anticipated his response.

"Well, typically we do—" I countered in my imaginary conversation, "in the theatre, that is, but this was a private party, postseason, and we had to manage ourselves."

Utter horseshit—but he knew no better. That should be enough, but my mind raced ahead anyway to give further credence to my story.

That was, of course, why I had forgotten it. Usually the costumers handled it, and I was not in the habit of dealing with it myself. *And that's that*, I thought and tried to let it go.

All the while trying to ignore the "why." The necessity of the lie in the first place. That I was a horrible person, wilfully intending to cheat on a decent man who was clearly infatuated with me.

That I didn't love him, that it was a relationship of convenience that I was intending to break off at a not far off—but as of yet, still ill-defined—future date offered me little solace. So instead, I tucked it away. I boxed it up and shelved in the attic in the back of my mind and focused on seeing Sebastian again.

Arriving back at the venue, I quickly scanned the room for James—then slowly reconnoitred the room for Sebastian. Lars must have seen me when I arrived and approached. As was customary when it was the two of us, he spoke in French.

"Stefanie! You guys were fantastic tonight! Really the best I've ever seen you dance it—but I thought you'd left."

"Well, I had, but . . . have you seen Sebastian? I bought him a performance gift and forgot to give it to him." Another lie.

Lars studied me with a knowing eye.

"Ash left about twenty minutes ago," he said before hesitating, apparently considering before going on. "Stefanie . . . Ash told me he won't be returning in the fall. He won't be renewing his contract."

"What!?" I said, dismayed.

"He's been offered a principal position in the Puget Sound Ballet, and an opportunity to choreograph his own work. It's more than we can offer, and it's really a great—"

"When is he leaving!?"

Lars took time to shake out a cigarette and light it. He drew deeply and exhaled. "Apparently he's flying out tonight."

Looking at Lars, without warning, tears began tumbling down my cheeks.

Sensing my fragility, Lars embraced me. "I know, Stefanie, I'm sorry."

That was the last time I saw Ash . . .

. . . That was seven years ago.

16
Prelude

Now . . .

After pouring us some more wine, Ash returned the bottle to the kitchen.

And it was then, there—I found myself again. Sitting on the sofa, gazing through the window. City lights in the darkness shone through gently falling snow. A glass of merlot in hand. Inside, only the dim flicker of Christmas lights. Lori Carson's "Snow Come Down" plays quietly in the background, the sound softly emanating from nowhere, matching my breaths in its slow cadence.

I hear the light fall of Ash's footsteps on hardwood as he approaches.

As memories of the loneliness begin to surface, the ache of that moment, I turned to him. "Why did you leave, Sebastian?" The words, unbidden, escape from me.

Seven years on, and the echo of that evening's abandonment still presses upon my heart.

"Why did you have to run away?"

And in the twilight's parting sweetness,
dusk drew its dying breath.

With hazel eyes of allure,
and emotionally without refuge,
Sebastian summons me . . .

"Will you dance with me now Stefanie?"

A moment passes . . .
Then another . . .
My hand finds his own,
and slowly,
into his embrace,
he enfolds me.

His left hand curling my right
against his heart.

At the small of my back,
his right,
ever so gently
finds its place.

Inching from his shoulder,

cambering towards his nape,
from shirt to skin,
my left hand finds purchase.

My fingertips exploring
where the curl of his hair
meets the soft of his skin.

Our foreheads lightly touching.
Turning . . . slowly turning,
we dance like this.

Our eyes reconnoitre
in the soft glow of lights,
searching one another,
as the music's rhythm subsumes us.

Then the room,
the lights,
the world falls away . . .

And what remains
is just the two of us . . .
the one of us.

Drawing him ever closer
with sweet hesitations,

our lips brush.

And with bites so tender,
I playfully tempt his lips.

And from the teasing,
delicate kisses blossom.

His fingers flow
through the fall of my hair,
while my ear is caressed softly
with the warmth of his whispers.

The slight scruff of his face upon my cheek,
my head reclining and bosom rising,
availing my décolleté
of his kisses silken.

And with each quickening heartbeat,
each sharpening breath . . .
my body's volition ever yielding,
when finally,
in surrender . . .
the yearning consumes us.

In his hand
he takes my own,

and following the faint flicker of Christmas lights . . .
I let myself be guided.

And in the dark of his room . . .
buttons loosened.

And in the soft of his bed . . .
garments unceremoniously fell to the floor.

And it is here,
in the night's quiescence . . .
we find our rhythm.

17
The Presage

That night, I dreamed I'm back in England. Motoring along the countryside in a convertible. I wonder idly to whom it belongs. Its redness contrasts with the green of the lush foliage rushing past.

The road ahead of me, ever-winding alongside a wide river . . . Then I'm standing on the precipice, gazing into its depths. The water, black and ominous, flows unceasingly below, lapping at its sides. A long bridge spans the banks. A gusting wind chills my skin.

On the far side, dressed in a classic suit, like something out of an old film, is Sebastian. He is calling to me. I hear his voice, but through the winds roar, I can't make out what he is saying.

Suddenly, the bridge begins to falter, pieces of it falling into the river's blackness below. My anxiety rising, I realise I'm running out of time. Behind me the convertible revs its engine, beckoning me . . .

18
Contentions

Saturday, December 14th

I awake to the sounds of an espresso machine, the smell of coffee, and Jasper, who having found his way under the comforter, is stretched long against my belly, warming me with his soft fur.

Ash enters the room with two cups, smiles, and kisses me softly on the forehead. "Sleep well?" he asks, and unsettling dream aside, I actually had. "I made you a latte—is whole milk okay?" he asks as he hands me a cup.

I nod, take a sip, and look at him—smiling shyly, but saying nothing. As I begin to come around, caffeine chasing away the last tendrils of sleep, I feel my emotional chaos return for an encore performance.

Jasper rolls onto his back, stretches his limbs, then relaxes with his feet still splayed in the air. I envy his respite while I stroke his belly.

Ash sits down on the edge of the bed and looks at me apologetically.

"Listen, Stefanie . . . I took your mobile from your purse," he says as he fishes it out of his pocket.

At first, it's just a notion in the back of my mind: a vague unease I can't quite articulate. Was he concerned about invading my privacy? Then my eyes open wide as I remember that the ring's in my purse—*Oh God, he's seen the ring!?* My mind, shifting gears, begins to race.

He couldn't have, I try and convince myself. *It was hidden in its case.*

But with my gears ever-churning, mechanistic logic draws the tragic, inevitable conclusion: *It was "hidden" in its Tiffany's, robin-egg blue, just the right size to hold a ring case.*

"I heard it buzzing," he continues, "and I think we may have forgotten about your . . . mom."

I stare at Ash blankly for a second. As his statement has no bearing on my ring chimera, it takes a moment to realise the implication, and then—

"Kut!"

Sitting bolt upright, the ring panic temporarily placed on hold (one emergency at a time), with one hand I reach for the phone, with the other I keep the comforter from slipping down. Alarmed, I looked to find multiple voicemails and innumerable texts.

I dialled quickly, before I had strategised what to say.

"Mum!?"

"Stefanie! *Waar ben je? Gaat alles goed met je?!*" (*Stefanie! Where are you, are you alright!?)*

"Yes—yes I'm fine. I'm so sorry I didn't call, but . . . Do you remember Sebastian?"

Silence—then, "Ash from the ballet? Of course."

"Well, Mum, you'll never believe it—we bumped into each other, Ash and me—in a bookshop! And once we started catching up, we must have lost track of time, because . . . well, we were catching up that is, and—"

"And now it's 7:45 in the morning," she finished.

Having no response, I bite my lip to endure the silence. And after a seeming eternity of waiting, she says—

"Well, as long as you're okay, Stefanie." I breathed an immense sigh of relief—then she said, "*Laat me met Ash praten,*" (Let me speak with Ash,)—and once again, the wind was immediately knocked out of me.

I looked at Ash and, not yet finding my voice, handed him the phone. As they speak, I bury my face in my hands, and began to unravel.

"Hello, Mrs. Janssen . . . Yes, of course, 'Sophia' . . . I did . . . She's fine, we're just having some coffee . . . Yeah, I'd love to. What time should we meet? . . . Okay, look forward to seeing you then."

"It appears we're brunching at the Edgewater with your mom," Ash said with a barely contained smirk. His impish grin, his "trying not to smile," smile.

I peek up from my hands as Ash brushes aside some hair that has fallen over my face. At his touch, it leaps out of me. He drops his smile and worry suddenly pervades his face. Full of concern, he sees I'm on the verge of tears.

"Stef!?" He holds me while I sob on his shoulder. His embrace is a warm refuge from my sins. An enclave of tenderness from the relentless torrent of my mind.

Suddenly, my shame beseeches me, and I pull away slightly in order to face him. His kind hazel eyes search me out: kindness I yearn for, but don't deserve.

"Sebastian, there is something I need to—"

"Shhh—" he whispered, placing his finger to my lips, silencing me.

"Stefanie . . . I don't want to know," he said, replacing his finger with a kiss.

I stare at him, listening, trying to control my breaths as my chest begins to pound.

"If you're married, I don't want to know."

I inhale sharply, my eyes tearing up.

"If you're engaged, or living with someone—I don't want to know. If there's a boyfriend, or if after today, we never see each other again—*I don't want to know that either.*"

"All I want to know, Stefanie, is that today, this moment . . . you love me. It isn't everything, I know," he said, lighting a cigarette, "but it's enough."

I take the cigarette from him, and holding his face in my

hands, tenderly kiss his lips. Warmth permeates from my abdomen to my extremities, pacifying me, soothing my mechanism, slowing the gears. And slowly, I draw him back into bed.

19
Encore

It comes faster this time, the driving, the river, standing near the edge, Ash across the expanse, motioning to me, his voice lost in the wind, the bridge faltering, my anxiety increases with the relentless passage of time, and the beckoning growl of the convertible ever calling me.

20
Machinations

I awake with a start. The clock reads 10:23 a.m. In a panic I ask, "Ash, what time did you say we're meeting Mum?"

Ash is curled in behind me, matching my contour, holding me.

"Mmmm, what time is it now?"

"10:23."

Ash opens an eye and peeks at his watch. "Ahh— about now."

"—Kut!" I spat for the second time that morning. And forgetting the comforter this time, I sat up and began to search for my clothes.

Ash laughs as he pulls on some jeans. "That's now officially my favourite word in the English language."

"It's Dutch," I mumble quietly, "and I didn't say it."

"Especially when you say it!" he went on, ignoring me. I smiled despite myself. Then, sighing, "Oh god, I need a

shower and some fresh clothes. All I have is what I wore on the plane. I can't go to meet Mum looking like a trollop."

While I'm dreading the encounter with Mum, the immediate dread of *being late* to the encounter with Mum has, for the moment, taken precedence. *One emergency at a time*, I remind myself.

"Stefanie," Ash says calmly. He places his hands on my shoulders as I pout and, "Lauren Bacall" style, look up to meet his gaze.

"Listen, we can shower here, and—where are you staying?" he asked.

"The Weston."

"Okay, we can take the Monorail right to the Weston. You can change clothes, and we'll take an Uber to the Waterfront. We'll be there in twenty—twenty-five minutes, I promise. Okay?"

"Okay," I said.

"And you are not a trollop," he said seriously. "You're my Stefanie."

I smile sheepishly.

"Now to be honest, I'm not entirely sure what the difference is," he said, teasing me now, "but together, I'm sure we'll figure it out."

"Tosser!" I glowered, not entirely convincingly, and threw a pillow at him.

"I'll get the shower going," said Ash, as he walked toward the bathroom.

"I don't think so, mister!" I said, racing past him, playful again and still naked. "I'm showering alone. You've caused quite enough trouble for one morning."

21
The Edgewater

Thirty-seven minutes later, our Uber dropped us off outside the Edgewater.

Mum had arrived early and seemed to be eagerly anticipating our arrival. Her head cocked to one side, she studied us as we made our approach.

Taking a deep breath and displaying as much gravitas as I can muster, I walked deliberately to her table, leaving Ash to follow—intentionally creating distance between us.

Ash must find this so amusing, I thought, feeling a tangled mix of angst and elation, imagining his trademarked impish grin as he trails along behind me.

After giving Mum a hug, I intentionally sit next to her, forcing Sebastian to take a seat across the table. A little remove, I reasoned, to help put a stop to any involuntary touching.

"Stefanie tells me you have your own company now?" asks Mum. "That must be exciting."

"Well, at the moment my 'company' is nothing more than a loose-knit group of former dancers who work entirely on my promise to pay them. So far we've had nothing like a regular season."

"And what steps are required to ensure you continue to move in that direction?" said Mum, ever the pragmatist.

"I'm writing grants, working on non-profit status, doing outreach. I'm waiting on a grant decision right now that would fund an entire season—*if we're approved.* Giving the bunheads classes is a huge part of it, as it's their parents who have the money."

"Honestly, I only sleep for about four hours a night. Sometimes I even nap at the studio."

"Stefanie's certainly has her share of sleeping difficulties," said Mum—perhaps oversharing. *Nevertheless*—I'm relieved by the conversation so far.

Then she says—

"Though I imagine you two got some better rest last night—"

"What sort of pieces are you working on!?" I blurt out, overcorrecting.

Ash twists his face to keep from grinning. "At the moment we're working on some contemporary pieces incorporating mime. I also have an idea for more of a major work 'Hilarion'—It's the story of Giselle told from Hilarion's point of view."

"How is that?" inquires Mum.

"I always felt that Hilarion got the short end of the stick. Sure, he's a bit rough around the edges, but at least he is honest, he did love Giselle, and he exposed that fraud Albrecht for what he is. But it's a lot of bodies, and the way I imagine it, far more production than I typically am up for. Also, it would be a lot more expensive to produce."

"Actually, that is what the major grant I mentioned would fund. I have a friend on the Arts Commission who has some weight, and he thinks we have a real shot, so hopefully it will go our way."

"It sounds as if you stay quite busy. So, tell me Ash," Mum asked, "Do you have time for—anyone special?"

"Noooo," answered Ash, then impersonating Alan Rickman, continued, "I'm afraid I have been tried and found to be romantically without merit, and thus, have henceforth been justly sentenced to a lonely life of Haagen-Dazs and romantic comedies."

"Oh brilliant! I love his voice!" said Mum. "I was so sad when I heard he'd passed."

Turning to me she said, *"Heb je dat gehoord, Stefanie? Ash is met niemand aan het daten."* (Did you hear that Stefanie? Ash isn't seeing anyone.)

Over-caffeinated and not at all hungry, I barely touch my food. Instead I fidget, talk nervously and too much, bouncing from one topic to another. And when I wasn't speaking myself, I was on high alert, ever ready to interrupt again if I sensed Mum going into a conversational area I wished to avoid.

But eventually, I must stop to breathe . . . and then it happens.

"Stefanie, did you tell Ash the news?" says Mum as indescribable panic begins to race through my body. "He must be allowed to congratulate you!"

All blood leaves my skin, my eyes go wide, and I realise I have stopped breathing. I want to redirect, to yell, to scream if need be, but as if in a nightmare, I'm in paralysis, unable to move.

"Oh, Ash it's wonderful news," said Mum. "Our little Stefanie here—*is having a piece choreographed on her!*"

I laugh nervously, and a little too loud. Hoping for the physical relief that should come soon but hasn't yet.

"Thomas Hargrove is coming to Santa Barbara to choreograph a piece especially for Stefanie," Mum continues.

"Good for you, Stef," Ash says. "I'm envious—Thomas never choreographed anything on me."

"He did so," I countered, finding my breath, recovering a little and giving my mind something to focus on. "He set *Carmen* on you." I relish the natural conversation, and begin to unwind.

"Don Jose, yes, but that was before he became famous," he adds.

"True, 'Carmen's' the piece that made his reputation," I say. "But anyway, choreographers never get famous—not in the American pop star way."

"Right," Ash said, "only in the Euro artsy-fartsy genre."

I laughed—genuinely this time.

"No, you are right," he continued, "or perhaps one dancer in a generation is known to the general public. Nureyev, Baryshnikov, Fonteyn."

Mum's ears picked up. "Tell me about Baryshnikov, Ash."

"Well, though I never met him, he was a huge influence on me. Thomas told me that when he came to the States, he set a very high standard of technique for male dancers. Really blew the lid off it."

Ash continued, "That's the good part; however, the ill-fated consequence of that was America started producing a lot of technical robots. Dancers who had excellent technique but were otherwise boring to watch, had no voice of their own and nothing to say. That's what Thomas wanted to correct. It was his 'raison d'être,' if you will."

I always warmed when Ash became passionate about his subject, and I momentarily forgot my precarious situation. "And now you have taken up the torch and run with it," I said genuinely.

Ash reddened a bit but continued. "Well—technique for technique's sake was a definite 'no-no' with Thomas. At its best, it only amounts to showing off. 'Technique,' he would say, 'must always be in-service of the dance.'"

"Sooo . . . tell me, Stefanie," said Mum.

My guard now lowered, I casually turned to face her.

"Do you two have plans for the rest of the day?"

Then, cocking her head to one side and looking directly at

me, she continues, "I imagine you two will probably want to do some more . . ."

Her eyebrows raise—

"*'Catching up!?'*— before our flight tomorrow."

I blush and stare at the table.

"So soon?" Ash asks.

I hear the slight distress in his voice, and I look up to find his concerned hazel eyes upon me. He is still smiling, but his smile no longer reaches his eyes. His hands reach across the table to find mine involuntarily, meeting them halfway.

"Well, I'll leave you to it then," Mum says as she stands. "*Ik had een eenpersoonskamer moeten nemen. Dan had ik geld bespaard*" (I should have saved money with a single room), she murmurs, though loud enough for me to hear.

"Ash—it was so nice to see you again." Mum means it; I can tell. And with that she is off.

Alone now, we sit. Our hands still holding. Saying nothing. The waitress asks if we would like anything else as she busses our table.

Then we both speak at once—again, and the absurdity of the repetition brings a quiet laugh from us both.

"Ash, I . . ." and I find I can't continue. So, I breathe and face him.

"Use your words, Stefanie," Ash says quietly.

I laugh a little, despite myself, but as I again meet his gaze, his eyes are grave, full of solemnity.

This is it—we're finally here. The inescapable has arrived. Empty and resigned, emotional gravity adheres me to my place. Surrendering to the moment, I feel strangely quiet inside, the relentless gears of my mechanism have slowed, finally grinding to a halt.

I take a deep breath and begin again, "Ash, I . . ." He listens and this time doesn't stop me, "Sebastian . . . I might be engaged."

He lifts his brows but says nothing.

"I was proposed to, and I guess I was taking the trip to think it over. So Ash . . . I need to—"

"Know if this was a last hurrah or . . . something more?" Ash finishes my sentence.

I sit silently. Watching. Waiting. Breathing.

"Stefanie, you have a kind heart, and I know you would rather avoid confrontation than hurt someone's feelings, especially mine. And that crazy mind of yours—one moment pointedly insightful, and the next distracted and lacking all common sense—I don't want to further distress you."

Inside my chest, my heart pounds on the walls to be let out.

"Stef . . . " Ash begins, but then he pauses, leans forward, and meets my eyes. He adjusts his hold on my hands like he used to do when we partnered.

"If we get the handhold right, the rest will follow," he would say.

"Stefanie," he begins again, his voice is lower, quieter, "Listen, if you leave—if you need that life I suspect awaits you—I'd completely understand. It's really been . . . Stefanie—seeing you again. I'll keep plugging away here, and of course, you'll always have my love—*always.*"

"But Stefanie," he continues, "if you stay—*and I so want you to stay*—you'd be choosing a guy who would rather live a happy life dead broke in a world of art than have all the money in the world and live in its absence. All I can offer you is an underwater mortgage, my as-of-yet unfunded company, and my witty repartee."

"And Jasper," I say quietly.

"There is Jasper," Ash repeats.

"Jasper is huge," I whisper through tears. "I saw him in your flat, and . . . we fell in love."

22
Polyphony & Discord

Arm in arm, we spent the afternoon strolling leisurely along the waterfront. At the ferry terminal, we decided to spend the day on Bainbridge Island, being tourists. My appetite returning, we stopped for a bit of nosh at the Harbor House.

On the return, we watch the sunset from the deck of the ferry before it gets too cold and we have to return inside the cabin for a snog and a snuggle.

As we walked through the Sculpture Park on the way back to Ash's flat, we stopped for a time near the amphitheatre to observe a winter wedding in progress.

"That poor bride must be freezing," I said, noticing her nuptial discomfort. "I wouldn't want to get married outside this time of year—not in Seattle, at least."

"So, when would you like to get married?" asked Ash.

His double entendre causes a smile to overtake me and I shoot him a furtive glance as I begin to warm from the inside.

As we continue our stroll up Western Ave, back to Ash's flat, he says, "Stefanie, about tonight—"

"Don't tell me you have a date!" I chided.

Ash shook his head slightly and chuckled, "I think you give me a lot more 'game credit' than I deserve. I was going to say, don't forget to call your mom."

I interpreted his statement as meaning "communicate in some fashion" and decided a text message was more than adequate.

"We're thinking of taking in a late show . . . Please don't wait up." I hit send.

As we continued our walk, taking a right on Denny, a left on Warren, I can't help but glance at my phone every thirty seconds awaiting a reply.

Finally, just as we reach his building it comes:

"See you tomorrow morning. Stefanie—Don't be late."

While relieved, I'm also more than a little peeved at myself.

For god's sake, Stef, you're an adult now, nearly thirty years old. How is it that woman still reduces me to adolescence?

First Variation

The shield of my conviction torn asunder.
Veracity cracks and splinters its facade.
My cirrus lies of white darken with thunder.
Must my marrow be inherently so flawed?

—Sleepless night Dec 15th, 3:25 a.m,

23
Consequence & Trepidation

Sunday, December 15th

If I were a writer, this is where I'd choose to end my tale. With romance blossoming, unrequited love at long last reciprocated, and genuinely happy forever after and ever more . . .

But it goes on . . . this life, and I was apprehensive about what lay ahead. For the demons of my past had not yet been lain to rest, and even decisions of the heart have their consequence.

The following morning, head down and eyes closed, I find myself havering outside the door of Mum's hotel room—rife with trepidation.

Taking a breath, I lift my head, stare intently at the number on the door, and pray to God, Jesus, Buddha, Allah, and *Fuck All* to calm my apprehension just a little.

It has not escaped my notice that I'm on the twenty-ninth floor—my age—and that it's a long way down. Would there be any poetry in that, I wonder? Any redemption?

Stop it, Stefanie!

I check my watch—again—then take a final breath, lift my chin, hiss an audible—

"Sod it!" and open the door.

Mum is there, suitcase on the bed. She is folding clothes, packing for the flight. She glances up, sees me, and returns to her work.

"Did you have a nice time?" she asks perfunctorily.

"Mum!" I say brightly, but my enthusiasm feels forced. "I'm thinking of staying in Seattle . . . a bit longer."

Mum purses her lips, nods, and continues to fold and pack, pack and fold, but says nothing.

Tentatively, I press on. "Just a week or so," I say, imbuing my voice with more inflection than I feel. "Ash is behind administratively, with the school and grants, and well—*everything really*. I can teach classes to free up time for him, and I have some ideas that could help the company!"

In the silent, bereft desolation that follows, I hear only the whispers of my mechanism's gnashing gears as I count my breaths awaiting a response . . . but Mum simply continues to pack.

Eventually . . .

"I see"

. . . is all she says.

Her words hang in the silence like daggers. Like an inevitable collision, they wait for only the precise moment to fall and inflict maximum damage. An auspicious beginning, it was not.

I sit down and contract myself into a smaller target. My hands find themselves over my belly in a protective gesture, the nails of one hand dig into the other as I hold my breath.

"So, help me understand," Mum continues humourlessly. "Sebastian's running behind, and you've decided to stay so you two can engage in some more . . . *'catching up?'* "

I close my eyes, exhale slowly, and steel myself for what *I know* will follow. Her forbearance at brunch is now entirely absent.

"Since you bumped into each other at the bookshop the other day, it seems you've been bumping into each other as often as possible."

Above me, blades begin quivering their macabre ballet of anticipation.

Just breathe, Stefanie.

"Tell me, Stefanie—don't you still have some unfinished business back home to attend to?"

I sigh, and without looking up, eventually manage . . .

"Maar ik hou niet van hem, Mum." (But I don't love him Mum.)

"Stefanie!" she says. I recoil inwardly as her tone sharpens and she turns to face me. "It makes no difference whatsoever—Marcus has been very kind to you and deserves better!"

Mum studies me silently—taking time to collect her thoughts before continuing.

"I'll give you a week," she declares. "I want you to be sure this time. And then I want you back next Saturday—to conclude things. And Stefanie—*no more lying.* Isn't Freddy in a program committed to rigorous honesty?"

"I never lied," I whisper, and *immediately* regret it.

Mum simply glares at me. I stare at the ground in her general direction, as I still can't meet her eyes. Her silence is worse than her scolding. Her incredulity—palpable. The room is thick with it.

"Good," she continues, finally breaking the silence.

"But it's best not to start now. Remember Stefanie, omission with intent to deceive . . . *is lying.* Remember that when you speak with Marcus."

I remain quiet and force myself to take another breath.

"Have you even phoned Marcus?"

"Mum!" I protest, finally looking up. While it would be no more than a minor concession on her part, on this point (at least), perhaps I could defend myself. "It's been only two days, and he knows where I am—"

"But not where 'you are,' Stefanie!"

Mum's voice thunders with rebuke. With a single vitriolic sentence, she unearths the substratum of my defences. Her wrath consumes all the oxygen in the room, and I struggle to even breathe.

"Do you even know yourself!? You carry an engagement ring given to you by a man who has no idea his 'bride to be' is off sleeping with an old flame!"

With meticulous precision, emotional daggers plummet down upon me in a hailstorm of malice, executing their purpose, their raison d'être: piercing and splintering the shield of my disgrace.

"Honestly, Stefanie—Did you really think you could *fuck* your troubles away!? *Wat bezielde je!?"* (What possessed you!?)

Shame wells up in my eyes and begins to trickle down my cheeks. I have nothing. I can only lower my head, close my eyes, breathe, and endure it. Contrition bleeds yellow from my wounds as tears fall from my face.

"Stefanie." Her voice is still firm, but softer now. "I support your decision. I always thought Marcus was a bit of an *achterlijke gladiool* (retarded gladiolus), and I've always been fond of Ash . . . *But you mustn't treat people like they're your playthings!* You can't just leave them on the ground like a discarded doll you've grown tired of!"

"Listen," she continues taking a breath, softer again, "you have your week—but you must call him. *Waarom niet nu*?" (Why not now?)

Though her inflection rose at the end, *it wasn't really a question.*

My body trembling, I force myself to stand and walk past her, when . . .

"And I see you have started smoking again."

Inhaling sharply, I close my eyes and stiffen mid-step as a final blade skewers me between the shoulder blades.

"Why don't you call him from the balcony? You can smoke out there if you like. *Twee vliegen in een klap.*" (Two flies with one swat.)

I drop my head and continue my "dead man's walk" to the balcony.

While light in my purse, the phone becomes increasingly heavy in my hand. I light a cigarette, close my eyes, and draw deeply. I stare at my mobile for an entire minute before I press dial and force the phone to my ear.

"Stefanie!" Marcus exclaims. "Did you have a nice time? You're flying back today, right?"

"Hi, Marcus." I do my best to keep the emotion out of my voice, but Mum's categoric castigation of my character *keeps . . . clamouring . . .* cacophonously—

Stop it, Stefanie! Stop and breathe.

I exhale, make an effort to let it go, and try to focus on the matter at hand. "About that, look . . . there is a new dance company starting up—"

"Did you pick up some more guesting work?" he interrupts.

"Yes, exactly," I say, but with Mum's presence radiating through the sliding glass door, I backtrack a bit. "Well— something like that, anyway. Look, Marcus, I'm going to be here a bit longer, but I'll be back next Saturday, and we can talk then, okay?"

"Next Saturday!? . . . Okay, well—I understand when duty calls, but I can't wait to see you again, Stefanie. We've got a lot going on down here, and I can't wait to show you!"

"Listen, Marcus, they are waiting for me in rehearsal." My fabrication, though effortless, is not without guilt. "I need to go."

"Go do your thing, Stef—remember I love you."

"Sorry, Marcus, but I have to run, everyone's waiting—bye."

Back in the room, Mum is waiting.

"I know this isn't easy for you, Stefanie." She is softer now, gentler. "And I know sometimes your heart gets in the way of your head. But it will continue to haunt you until you deal with it. It's no way to start anew."

Grudgingly, and not without resentment, I admit to myself she is right. Still, thinking of it fills me with foreboding nonetheless.

Mum lifts my chin with her hand and looks me in my eyes. Gently she says, *"Onthoud dit, Stefanie. Na regen komt zonneschijn.* (Remember Stefanie, after the rain, the sun will shine.) Please, enjoy your week, and say goodbye to Ash for me."

And with that—I'm excused. My presence—if not my behaviour.

My stay of execution granted, I leave the hotel. An enormous weight, for the moment at least, has been lifted from my shoulders. As my wounds begin to heal, I wonder idly how she knew I'd been smoking.

24
Quandary

I exit the lobby, walk up 5th Ave, and take a right. In a cafe, sitting on a stool, latte in hand, Ash is waiting for me.

"How did it go?"

Seeing Sebastian brings on a fresh wave of emotion. He embraces me as I put my head on his shoulder.

"That good, huh?"

I grab a napkin, dab my eyes, and blow my nose. Determined not to waste another moment, I begin to pull myself together.

"Epic scolding . . ." I manage after a moment. My voice constricts up an octave as I continue, "Quite Damoclesian, really—but I'm here through next Saturday."

Sensing I'm not finished, Ash waits patiently.

"I was reduced to a ten-year-old this time—I think it's a new record. Apparently you're in love with a little ten-year-old slag, so good on you."

"Stefanie . . ."

Ash tries to console me. But I raise a hand. "No—I'll deal with it on Saturday," and looking in his eyes, "*I will*—but now we have things to do."

"Here," Ash says, handing me a latte, "maybe this will help."

"Talk to me Ash," I implored, "tell me about the company, about the challenges, about anything. *Please*—just give my mind something to focus on."

"I don't know where to start."

"Just start talking—*please!*"

Ash takes a breath and collects his thoughts.

"Well, in addition to what I mentioned at brunch, maybe the worst part is the scheduling. If I had money to pay, it would be a different story, but as it is, I need to accommodate the work schedules of the dancers—day care, in some cases.

"Sometimes they bring their babies, so I have a play area taking up floor space. Nothing says professional like a bunch of big plastic baby toys in the studio. I'm always worried a member of the board will drop by . . . Oh, that's right," he says slapping his forehead, "we don't have a board!"

"Then there is renting the studio space," he goes on, "in addition to all the choreography, still trying to dance myself. Finding performance venues, doing outreach . . ." Ash shakes his head. "I'm stretched pretty thin most of the time, and if the grant funding doesn't come through, it may be all for naught. I try and keep checklists, and a positive attitude, but it's all getting to be a bit much. Honestly, Stefanie, I think about throwing in the towel every other day."

He sighs. "In my mind, I imagined choreographing my own work and setting pieces on friends especially for them, to showcase their talents. I never imagined all the bureaucracy and paperwork. I'm just a dumb dancer, Stef. What the hell was I thinking?"

25
Epiphany

After a few moments of sitting in silence, slowly sipping our lattes, with the dull commotion of cackling customers, coffee machines, and Christmas songs sounding sonorously in the background, an idea presented itself . . .

"Ash—you need Zoe! She should be your ballet mistress. Think of it!" I said, becoming more excited as the inspiration blossomed. "She could remember all the choreography, run the rehearsals, give the bunheads their classes and probably help administratively as well. Not to mention, she'd sure be a big hit at fundraising events—with the wealthy males, at least."

"The women too, once they saw how guileless she is," added Ash.

"Word," I said, suppressing a laugh.

Ash turned to me and stared.

"Really!? — *'Word?'* It's time for you to go back to England. Who are you, and what have you done with Stefanie?"

Ash was thinking. He started to protest, then thought some

more. He nodded and made little movements with his head while he deliberated. He liked the idea, though; I could see the connections in his mind starting to fire.

After a bit more silence, Ash began to nod acceptance.

"I need Zoe," he said. "Is she still in America? Is she still dancing herself? You two are about the same age, right?"

"Yeeesss . . ." I drew it out. "A couple months apart. We're both few years away from the big 'five oh.'"

"Uh-oh," said Ash, "I sense a wicked rejoinder coming."

"And this makes you how old?" I goaded. "Perhaps it's time to cut up an adult diaper to stuff in front of your dance belt to help with incontinence? At least it would help make your 'area' appear larger."

"Stefanie, nothing's going to help my 'area' appear larger . . ." Ash said; then he paused and reflected for a moment. "I may want to rephrase that."

"You know it's funny," Ash went on, "I was thinking about her the other day. I picked up a copy of *The Tao of Pooh*—do you remember that book?"

"That's Zoe! She never struggles. She sort of just saunters her way through life, having one adventure after another, and is always happy."

26
Ten Years Prior

When Zoe arrived at Capital City Ballet, it was a more than a breath of fresh air for me. She was a sent-from-heaven gift; allow me to explain.

At nineteen, I was hired at CCB from outside the companies ranks—"over and above" the existing women in the company as the new principal female lead and, it must be said, as "prima ballerina" in all but title.

In addition, I'm British and grew up speaking with a so-called "posh" accent, which unfortunately tends to become more marked if I'm feeling set upon.

"Stuck up" and "conceited" were the "not quite" out-of-earshot terms employed by my fellow ballerinas—that, and lesser synonyms.

I don't speak this way to sound superior, and I hardly sound like a Royal; it was just the environment I grew up in. Everyone spoke this way.

Though, if I'm to be completely honest, growing up, I may have sharpened it even further to distance myself from

Mum's Dutch-flavoured English, which, I shamefully admit, did occasion some embarrassment on my part as teenager.

Well, needless to say, that while I got on famously with the men, the women in the company never particularly warmed to me.

Then, like a beam of sunlight piercing through an arctic storm, arrived Zoe.

With both of us being foreign, and Zoe being Zoe, we took to each other immediately. She, more than anyone else, became my confidant. And finally, I had a girlfriend to talk to.

With a swashbuckling smile, Zoe's bohemian nature and friendly broad Aussie also helped pave the way for me to being at first tolerated, then accepted, and finally having some friendly relationships with the other girls myself.

If Zoe likes her, maybe she can't be all bad, I imagine was the collective notion floating through their minds.

Never judgmental and always supportive, on occasion Zoe wouldn't hesitate to caution me, usually relationship-wise, if she felt it necessary.

Zoe was always so . . . amazingly herself! She was "So Zoe" that playing around with affectionate names, I nearly went with Zózo, when the warmer and more feminine Zóza flowered in my imagination. She's been Zóza to me ever since.

Zoe, for her part, decided to find an affectionate name for me as well, and it didn't take her long to arrive upon "Stevie," which I love, and which I hope is a reference to Stevie Nicks, whom she adores.

Though, it must be said, she's also a huge fan of Stevie Ray Vaughn.

Preferring the etymology of the former over the latter, I decided to leave it at that, and didn't inquire further.

Zóza and I began to regularly critique each other's dancing. What started out as ad hoc dance advice began to turn into full on technique marathons. She had the ability to see what was technically going wrong in a dancer's turns, balancing, partnering or otherwise.

For my part, I was able to assist her in adding some dynamism to her movements and dramatic subtleties, and to bring out her acting voice.

Over time, as new prospects offered themselves and new adventures beckoned, it became time to leave CCB. And once again, escaping the long grasp of Mother, I fled, to of all places, *Texas.*

Fearing my arrival in the "Lone Star State" could be even less welcoming than it had been in California, I would have begged Zoe to come with me, but as it turned out, we left together, becoming both flatmates and principals in Austin's Rainey Street Dance Theater.

And after several good years there, one Sunday afternoon, my mobile rang . . .

27
Overture

"Hello?"

"Yes, I'm calling to speak with a Stefanie 'Yan-se' and or a Zoe Bryne," said an extremely posh gravelly voice—apparently attempting a Dutch pronunciation of my name, and not doing too bad a job of it.

"This is Stefanie, and 'Janssen' is fine. May I ask what this is regarding?"

"My name is Ambrose Thornhausen, and I'm the director of the Montecito Ballet near Santa Barbara. I was in Austin recently and saw the two of you's performance of *Duet*. Simply put—you were stunning! Both of you. And performed with such intimacy. I dare say I've been imagining the two of you together ever since! Err . . . eh, *dancing*, of course."

I smiled inwardly at both at his intention and his redirection.

Duet was a piece Zoe and I had choreographed ourselves. It consisted of a number of little vignettes illustrating various aspects of our relationship in dance form. We had to come up with it in a hurry to replace a scheduled piece where the two intended dancers had taken a bad fall while attempting a lift during rehearsal.

Zoe was prepared, as ever, to step in to cover the female role, but the men were either too spooked, or didn't feel they had enough time to adequately prepare. Interestingly enough, though we threw it together in a couple of afternoons, it was quite well received and went on to become a staple of RSDT's repertoire.

"I used to dance with Lars Lavigne back in the day," Ambrose continued. "He gave you two the highest recommendations. I know this is a bit out of the blue, but I was curious if I could lure you two to come perform it as guest artists here in Santa Barbara."

"We have a small summer season here. You'd have accommodations. I have a lovely guest house, so you would have some autonomy. We may be able to supply a per diem as well, in addition to your guesting fees. And of course—well, let's start with that."

"I'm flattered," I said. "I've never been to Santa Barbara. But Zoe's out at the moment. She should be back—at some point, and I would need to speak with her about it."

"Of course. Listen, perhaps I could interest you in the three of us having a late-night rendezvous . . . *to eh, discuss details and such."*

I found his faux pas—if that's indeed what they were—both amusing and oddly charming. And despite myself, I couldn't keep from grinning.

"Would that be possible?" Ambrose continued, "I hate to

pressure you, but I need to finalise something rather urgently. When you do you expect her back?"

"Well—"

That depends if she is reading not.

"I'm not entirely sure," I continue. "I'd hate to set up something and then not have her show for it."

"I tried to call her myself, left a message, but didn't get an answer," Ambrose replies.

She's definitely reading.

"It might be better if we call you," I said. "Would that be all right? Zoe should be back by nine our time, or she will call if she has plans."

"Yes, that would be fine."

After we became flatmates, we sampled Zóza's bell to her mobile for her to use as both a ringtone when I called, and an alarm. It goes off at a certain time so she will remember to come home or call me or just make contact; otherwise, I'd end up worrying.

"So," I continued, "how about in the range of seven to nine?"

"Excellent!" replied Ambrose. "And if for some reason I don't pick up, I'll call you right back. Thank you so much! And I shall be eagerly anticipating our three-way later this evening—*eh . . . conference call,* that is."

"Sure," I said, stifling a laugh, "I look forward *to speaking with you* later."

As I hang up the phone, I hear Zoe's VW Beetle pull into the driveway. She walks in through the front door carrying some Indian takeout.

"We might need to warm this a bit," she says apologetically, crinkling her nose. "I started reading while waiting for the food—sorry, luv."

"Zóza," I asked, "have you ever been to Santa Barbara?"

As Zoe saunters towards me, a Zóza smile spreads wide across her face, with those gorgeous brown eyes of hers looking right through me.

Tilting her head to one side she asks, "When do we leave?"

28
Ambrose

A week later, Zoe and I arrived in Santa Barbara. Ambrose had arranged for a limo to pick us up from the airport and shuttle us to his home for introductions. Meeting us in the foyer, he was sixtyish, bald, and podgy but also polite, witty, shrewd, and in possession of a marked self-confidence.

After too short a tour of his extensive home, we made our way out to his veranda to discuss the performance venue when a svelte young woman, impeccably dressed, emerged from the shadows.

"Ahh, lovely, and just in time. Allow me to introduce my wife, Anastasiia Mykolayivna."

Appearing at least thirty years younger than Ambrose, wearing a tailored outfit exposing her midriff, elegant, refined, and not a hair out of place, Anastasiia Mykolayivna appeared to have stepped off a runway.

"Please, call me Nastya," she said demurely in a lightly accented English. "It's very nice to meet you. Ambrose is overjoyed you have decided to come."

"Well, look at this," mussed Ambrose. "The four of us standing in the middle of California, and not one of us American!"

Nastya's phone began to ring. She glanced down at it and sighed. "I'm so sorry, it's the board calling, I must take this. Please excuse me. It was so nice to finally meet you. Perhaps we can lunch this afternoon, once you're finished talking shop?"

And as serendipitously as she had appeared, Nastya once again faded into the shadows.

After an awed moment of silence, Zoe remarked, "Your wife is *stunning*," giving voice to my thoughts as well.

"It's good to have money," said Ambrose, a contented gleam in his eye. "She's from Ukraine you know. With all the documents, visas, and bureaucracy—getting married was more of a bother than buying a house!"

From somewhere inside the house, we hear Nastya euphoniously respond, *"Ya vzhe kazav tobi, Ambrouz, diamant - dorohotsinna znakhidka!"*

Ambrose glanced with amusement in the direction of her voice before leaning into us. With a smirk planted on his face, he whispered, "Honestly, if I had to do it over again—*I'd probably just smuggle up a Mexican."*

Despite a near-heroic effort on our part at political correctness, Zoe and I were unable to keep ourselves from laughing, though I don't think either of us could have said exactly what we were laughing at.

I think it was the unexpected oddity of his remark as much

as anything that was so amusing. Was this a comment on his wife? Ukrainians? Mexicans? What an oddly intriguing sense of humour.

Ambrose, seeing he was on a roll, kept it coming, when a gorgeous young Latina girl of perhaps seventeen glided up behind him.

With almond-shaped eyes and colour to match, her jet-black hair undulated down well past her waist and tossed gently in the breeze. Barefoot, bikini topped, and with a towel wrapped about her waist, her olive skin glowed in the early morning sun.

She smiled warmly as she leaned into Ambrose, who embraced her causally without missing a beat. A smirk was planted on her face as she waited for him to finish.

"You know," he chuckled, "the best thing about having a European wife is when you send them to the store to pick up some hamburger, buns, and cheese—and they return with ground veal, brioche, and gouda!"

"How was the beach?" said Ambrose, turning to greet her. "Stefanie, Zoe, please meet my daughter, Constance— Christina, Gabriela De Lucia Flores."

"¡Por favor Papa!" she said, a little abashed, while graciously extending her hand. "There will be quiz before you go," she joked. "Papa's into titles. 'Connie' is fine. I'm here visiting for the summer."

Zoe and my ears perked up to hear a familiar soft friendly RP emanating from her when she spoke.

"Apologies for Papa's maverick sense of humour, but I'm afraid you'll just have to get used to it. There's simply no stopping him once he gets going."

Connie and Ambrose converse in Spanish for a moment; then she turned back to us and said, "You must be hungry after your flight. Nastya mentioned that perhaps the four of us could lunch? If you'd like to eat soon, I'll get changed. I just wanted to say hello. Papa's been talking so much about the two of you. I look forward to speaking with you more this afternoon."

She kisses him affectionately on the cheek before returning to the house.

"Oh, she's a tough one, that girl. Doesn't cut me any slack," Ambrose said proudly as he watched her walk away. And perhaps tinged with the slightest bit of nostalgia he added, "Just like her mother."

Zoe and I looked at each other with raised eyebrows, silently acknowledging our mutual intrigue. We were now both eagerly anticipating lunch to discover the backstory on this eclectic family.

29
Girls Only

"Las chicas necesitan un poco de espacio Papa," said Connie.

I closed my eyes and let the reverberation of Connie's Spanish tickle my ears. Had I only taken Mum's advice—but as it was, the end did sound a bit like the Italian for "a little space."

"I'm sorry, Amvrosiy, Connie's right," said Nastya as she straightened his tie and kissed him on the cheek. "It's going to be a 'girls only' lunch I'm afraid."

"But of course it is," replied Ambrose, opening the limo door for us and performing a low bow as we climbed in.

"And besides," continued Nastya affectionately, "I believe you've humoured our guests quite enough for one day."

"My princess, if it embellishes your afternoon's *divértiseman,"* said Ambrose, hand to his heart, "then so shall it be."

He closed the door before popping his head through the open window, and in a low growl whispered furtively, *"But be sure you don't leave out any of the tasty details,"* making us all giggle like schoolgirls.

30
Paseo Nuevo & the T-Shirt Covenant

"My mother passed away when I was six, and Papa raised me by himself for the next seven years, until I went off to school."

We lunched under an umbrella outside a cafe on State Street across from the Paseo Nuevo. The whitewash of the buildings, the red-tiled sidewalks, and a warm pleasant breeze all contributed to my growing infatuation with the area.

Is it possible to fall in love with a city?

"Are you in school now?" asked Zoe.

"Currently I'm at uni, studying linguistics at Oxford—it's where Tolkien taught, so I thought it a good fit."

"How many languages do you speak?" I asked.

"English, Spanish—a little Ukrainian now," Connie smiled at Nastya, "but linguistics is really a multifaceted discipline. Though, in essence, it's probably accurate to say it's concerned about how languages actually function rather than acquiring a lot of languages, or—another misconception—that it's about learning word histories."

The women's graceful lines prompted my next question.

"Do either of you dance?"

"No!" replied Connie, "I'll stick with Pilates, thank you very much."

Nastya, however, turned inward and fell silent. After a few moments she looked to us, nodding slowly. "I did," she said, and returned to her silence.

I glanced over at Zóza, but she was in her zone, a statue, so completely transfixed upon Nastya, I turned back to her myself.

Nastya closed her eyes, turned her face into the sunlight, and breathed deeply. Then she smiled and took a sip of her latte before continuing.

"I had—how do you say it? Teacher troubles. She was a disgraced ballerina from the Bolshoi. Never satisfied with her own career, she was determined to make the lives of her students as miserable as her own.

"And to that end, and that alone, was she truly exceptional. Her name was Ekaterina Katanskaya, or as we called her, Ekaterina Khtoznayevna Katastrofa."

Nastya twisted her lips deciding on a translation. "A . . . misbegotten catastrophe," she said finally.

"Misbegotten?" I asked, trying to get a better sense of it.

"She means bastard," Connie interjected. "It's a patronymic play on words—literally, daughter of 'who knows?'—which, by implication, speaks to the proclivities of her mother."

Then, smiling at Nastya, she continued, "You're far to well-bred for the English language, Nastya."

"Thank you, Connie," Nastya smiled, "our entire class probably lost 100 kg due to stress over body image. Every morning we stood in a line, and one by one we faced *'mashtab strazhdan'*—the scale of suffering."

"If we were deemed overweight—even by a gram—more than once a month, she would threaten to rescind our scholarships. Needless to say, we went to some pretty extreme measures," Nastya continued. "A friend of mine ate only apples for an entire month. Another girl, who I wasn't so close with, went to the extreme of eating only . . ." she turned to Connie and asked a question in Spanish.

"Condiments," answered Connie.

"Eating only condiments," Nastya finished.

Open-mouthed, Zóza and I gaped at each other.

"She was on a condiment diet!?" I exclaimed.

Zoe closed her eyes, sighed, and buried her shaking head in her hands.

"I was becoming bulimic myself, when one horrible over-worked morning, weak and undernourished, she kept forcing my turnout until I ended up with my kneecap—" Nastya gestured to the outside of her leg, where I noticed light scarring from corrective surgery was still visible, "over here."

"Oh my god, Nastya!" said Zoe, *"you poor thing!"*

"It was enough for me," Nastya exhaled, letting it go

when she suddenly sat back up. "It's not like that here, by the way!"

"No—Papa wouldn't have it—not at all. He's very protective of his dancers," added Connie.

"Anyway," Nastya continued, "now I dance Argentine tango with Ambrose. He's actually quite light on his feet, and he never fails to enter without a rose between his teeth."

As the four of us continued chatting and getting to know each other, I wondered to myself the best way to phrase the obvious question when, undeterred by formality, Zoe just came out with it.

"Connie, were you surprised by— "

"Me?" Nastya laughed.

"Not really—why would I be?" said Connie. "Papa's always had an eye for the ladies. I mean, I understand it may look a bit odd, but Papa's a good man and a wonderful father, so why wouldn't I want him to find a beautiful, intelligent companion?"

"As for me," said Nastya, "I'll admit I was a little hesitant at first, and I certainly wasn't looking for a 'sugar daddy' relationship, but his wit and charm eventually won me over, and he has such a unique sense of humour."

"We've noticed!" I laughed.

"How did you meet?" asked Zoe.

"The internet—though don't tell my parents that. And after a few months of Skype and emailing and so forth, one day, out of nowhere, he just appeared."

"Do tell!" implored Zoe.

"It was our usual Skype time, but on this particular day when Ambrose called, he said he 'just happened' to be in Poltava! He claimed he was on a layover from Amsterdam on his way to Paris. I told him that that the international airport was in Kyiv, and anyway, Poltava had to be at least 2,500 kilometres out of the way. He just shrugged his shoulders and mumbled something about the declining quality of the airlines these days, but as he was here anyway, would I be available for dinner? And, well, to make a long story short, the rest is history."

"Nastya, what did you say to him from inside the house?" asked Zoe—for both of us.

"I overheard him start in with his usual jokes and decided to remind him that a true diamond is a precious find," smiled Nastya. "We all tease each other a lot."

I warmed at this, and memories of my time teasing with Sebastian at CCB.

"In fact," Nastya continued, "he's always teasing me that some day he is going to write a guidebook: *The Proper Care and Feeding of your Ukrainian Wife*," she laughed.

"It's *The PC&F of your Latina Daughter* version for me," added Connie, shaking her head.

"I heard you speaking Spanish with your father, Connie. So does he speak Ukrainian as well?" I asked the both of them.

"Papa spent a lot of time in Spain growing up," answered Connie. "We have family there as well as Mexico, which is where my mother's from."

"As for Ukrainian," offered Nastya, "he's learning. But before deciding to get married and move to America, I made him memorise two sentences. The first is *'Ya tebe kokhayu,'* which means 'I love you,' and which he is to recite to me every day. And the second is—"

At this point, Connie started chuckling.

"Mstyva zhinka hirsha za dyyavola!"

Nastya paused, smiling, as we now, rapt with attention, waited for her translation.

"A vindictive woman is worse than the devil."

Zóza threw her head back and howled.

"Ohhh!" I yelled. "I like the way you think!"

"I'm putting that on a T-Shirt!" said Zóza.

"Can you say that Spanish, Connie?" I asked.

"Una mujer vengativa es peor que el diablo.'"

"Yes! We absolutely need T-shirts with that in every language!" I exclaimed.

We all laughed, and once we had settled down, Connie posed the question: "Well . . . do you really want to? I mean, why not?"

We looked back and forth at each other, and then Zoźa said, "Let's do it! But we need to get some hats too!"

"After all," intoned Nastya, "the importance of accessorising shouldn't be trivialised."

Needless to say, Zoe and I never returned to Texas, instead finding a new home and a new family for ourselves in Santa Barbara.

And with me having returned to 'The Golden State,' Mum's own relocation to Santa Barbara was but a matter of weeks.

31
Seattle

Now . . .

I took the last sip of my latte before relating news of Zoe to Sebastian.

"The last year or so Zóza's been *'Down Under'* visiting family," I said. "Remember, it's summer in Australia, and she has a baby of her own now—"

"Zoe's a mom!?" Ash asked, surprised.

"Since Aug 30th, and apparently her baby's as good-tempered as her mother."

"Heaven help us! Just what the world needs, a mini Zoe!" laughed Ash. "Do we know who the father is? Does she know? Immaculate conception? Seriously with Zoe, the possibilities are wide open."

"I do know," I replied, "more or less, but I think that's a tale for Zoe to tell."

"Fair enough, but—I mean, should I be buying two tickets to

the States? And before we get ahead of ourselves—do you think she'd even be interested?"

Ash is excited, I can tell.

"One ticket," I say, "and if I know Zoe, she is both ready for a change and up for the challenge."

"What's her baby's name?"

At this, my face lights up, and I can't hide my glee.

"Serafina Stefanie Bryne!" I exclaim, "I'm her godmother!—or I will be. We wanted to have a little ceremony to make it official. I haven't met her in person yet . . ."

My elation wanes with my words, when—just for a moment— I find myself immersed in a fjord of lament—treading darkness in the childless melancholy of an unwed thirty year old. ". . . Haven't had the chance to hold her," I manage to finish.

"Will this ceremony involve the two of you dancing naked in the moonlight?" smirks Ash, disrupting my dolour.

Finding a suitable response to Sebastian's well-timed jibe acts as a beacon, leading me back to shore.

"Stefanie?"

"The details—Sir Ash," I retort matter-of-factly, shaking it off, "have not been entirely decided. But you are more than welcome to live in hope."

Back on solid ground, the entire episode is over before it really began.

"Sorry, go on. I'm listening."

"She did barre through most of her pregnancy," I continued.

"With her baby about four months now, I imagine she has started back up. She never mentioned quitting to me."

"You know," I continued, "Zoe doesn't struggle like some of us . . . the rest of us."

"Zoe is a fucking force of nature," Ash said.

32
Reunion with Zóza

Thursday, December 19th

"Let's take Zoe to lunch when she arrives, plane food is terrible," I suggested.

"Stef, she is flying in from Sydney. That's a hell of a long flight, not to mention she'll probably be jet-lagged. We should probably just let her sleep."

"I'll bet you lunch she'll be ready for adventure," I wagered, "and it's Melbourne. Her family's from Tasmania."

"Zoe's from Tasmania!?" Ash chuckled, shaking his head.

"Originally, yes—near Kettering, if I'm not mistaken."

"*Kettering!?* Of course she is!—Why does that not surprise me? Okay you're on!" Then, mumbling to himself, "Welcome to Tasmania, home of the Unidentified Flying Ballet."

We waited expectantly at the international gate, looking down the escalator as the new arrivals made it past customs. Eventually, a platinum-blond woman with a familiar bob holding an infant in one arm and simultaneously drawing her luggage with the other—and doing both without the slightest difficulty—emerged from around the corner.

Despite a twenty-hour flight, holding and caring for an infant the entire time, Zoe stepped off the plane looking as effervescent as ever; I knew I'd won, of course, even before I saw her.

"Fucking force of nature," whispered Ash, shaking his head, conceding defeat.

I looked at Ash and smirked a victory smirk.

As Zóza sauntered closer, I saw that she still carried a small amount of baby weight, which—not surprisingly for Zoe— happened to have settled in all the right places.

I squinted up at Ash and saw this fact had not escaped his notice.

"Ash—stop looking at her boobs!" he did not respond, *"Ash!?"*

"I'm sorry, Stef," he teased, not turning away. "Did you say something?"

I hit him playfully in the stomach with the back of my hand. "Wanker."

"She looks like a damn fine smoke," Ash ruminated.

"What?"

"Round, firm, and fully packed."

"Do you want a severe beating!?"

"Come here," he said and pulling me in. He wrastled me

about slightly, burying his face in my hair and kissing me on the head.

I wasn't actually jealous, not of Zoe, but that didn't stop me from trying for a little more good-natured attention. "If Zoe's a force of nature—then what am I?" I said, crossing my arms and acting insulted.

He turned to me, more seriously than I expected.

"Stefanie, for me, watching you dance is like seeing *poetry in motion*. Do you think Zoe, even with all her gifts, could ever dance the Tango as competently as you?"

As I was expecting, more verbal jousting; his sincerity caught me off guard. My heart skipped a beat and I had to take a breath.

"Still though," Ash said, returning to his object, "you have to admit she looks gorgeous."

With total sincerity, and not the slightest amount of enmity, I admitted, "Yes, she does."

And then, prodding him further, "You know, I'm surprised you and Zoe were never an item."

"What! Me and Zoe? Stefanie, I love Zoe, but more like a little sister. Honestly, for me she was guileless to the point of being, well, not sexually intriguing."

"Uh huh." I intoned doubtfully, then goading him further and whispering in his ear . . .

"I think you were just afraid she'd read in bed!"

At once, Ash "spit takes" the coffee he was sipping.

Laughing and sputtering, he turns to me, covering his mouth and trying to recover. I'm happy to report that I caused some coffee to spew out his nose.

"I thought you were a proper English girl!" he stammers.

"Sorry, no," I say matter-of-factly, shaking my head, "I'm Dutch."

"Stevie!" Zoe exclaimed as she stepped off the escalator. Her baby was awake and looking about happily.

"Hey there, Zóza," I say, giving her an affectionate embrace before I hold her face in my hands and kiss her on the lips. Having Zoe back in my life was like being wrapped in a warm blanket.

"Oh! And who is this!?" I exclaim, brushing away some tears and turning my attention to her baby. "Oh Zóza, she's beautiful!"

The fact that Serafina looked like a Zoe in miniature—the same big brown eyes, even the same expression—only tugged on my heart strings and endeared me to her further.

"Can you say hello to your Aunt Stefanie? I have a feeling she's going to spoil you rotten." Zoe offers me Serafina: a gift I gladly accept. "Say hello to your niece, Stevie."

"Oh, I am never letting you go ever! Never ever!"

With Serafina in my arms, Zoe and Ash embrace as well.

"Sooo—" Zoe said, smiling radiantly, first turning excitedly to one of us, then the other, "What do we do now?"

"We're meeting Freddy for lunch," I say, never diverting my attention from little Stef.

"Freddy's here! Yeah!" she exclaims.

"How does Freddy know about lunch?" asks a confused but mostly recovered Ash.

"I phoned him last night and told him to meet us at Anthony's."

"But, how did you know Zoe would be up for it?"

"Of course I'm up for it," remarked Zoe. "I didn't even have brekkie on the plane!"

* * *

As Sebastian handled the rest of the luggage, I cradled Serafina in my arms as Zóza and I walked ahead.

"Sooo, Stefanie," Zoe inquired, *"tell me . . ."* Zoe had a way of saying much with few words.

While Ash trailed behind us, I spoke Dutch to Zoe.

Years ago, back in Capital City, Zoe was fascinated when she found out I spoke Dutch. I taught her a little, but finding I lacked pedagogical skills, eventually I just ended up buying her a Dutch language course for Christmas one year.

I had completely forgotten about it until a couple of months later when Mum came for a visit. We were having lunch, the three of us, when Mum made a barbed comment in Dutch regarding the mental capacity of our waitress . . . *and Zoe laughed.*

"Do you speak Dutch, Zoe?" asked Mum.

"I feel funny speaking it—I have such an Aussie accent and the sounds are difficult for me—but I . . ." Zoe bobbed her head a bit from side to side, "but I think I get the gist okay."

Mum, who had up to this point tolerated Zoe as my friend, but still felt she was a bit of a ditzy blond, proceeded to test her by questioning her in Dutch. Zoe responded in her broad Aussie. To say she got the gist was a bit of an understatement.

Later, Mum asked me further about Zoe's Dutch. I told her about the course I had bought her for Christmas.

"Not this last Christmas?"

"Yes."

"But it's only just March!" said Mum.

I then *gleefully* proceeded to relate her other talents as well. I don't think I've ever been *so happy in my life* as to see Mum, for once, so completely taken aback. And by my best friend!

Needless to say, Mum accorded Zoe far more respect after that.

"Speak woman!" said Zoe, bringing me back to the present.

"Nou, ik ben afgelopen vrijdag met Mum meegegaan—" (Well, I flew up with Mum last Friday and—")

"Ohh, Stevie!" said Zoe. "I'd almost given up on you two. And so—what happened with Marcus?"

I looked at her and squished up my face up a bit.

"Ahh . . ." Her eyes took on a look of concern. "So, there is *still that.*"

I nodded, "Mum's being—" I started

"A relationship Nazi?" Zoe finished.

"Well—that's a bit much—for a Dutch person that is, but . . . well, maybe a little."

Zoe pulls my head to her and kisses me on the temple.

"I love you, Stevie," she says, "and so does Mum."

I lay my head on her shoulder, and with Serafina asleep in my arms, I wonder, not for the last time, if a child is in my future as well, and we continue our leisurely stroll to the car.

33
Confessions at Anthony's

Freddy spotted us from the waiting area of Anthony's Bell Street Diner, and wearing a big smile, walked over to our booth. While he had grown a bit of a paunch in the belly, his face had matured handsomely. An elf still, certainly—but a wise elf.

We stood to greet him, and Zoe, having heard some of his recent history from us on the ride from the airport, gave him an extra-long embrace.

"Hey Bell," said Freddy affectionately as he hugged her and kissed her on the cheek.

After introductions to Baby Stefanie, posing for a few "Chrissie pickies" as Zóza would say, and a little small talk . . .

"Freddy!" said Zoe with that completely receptive, non-filtered emotionality she had.

She took Freddy's hands from across the table.

"Tell me, I want to know . . . how are you?"

Stretching out her words, she intimated far more than she said.

Intuiting it was time to tell his tale, Freddy looked down at the table for a moment, took a breath, then looked back up.

"Well—I suppose like all good stories, it begins with *'there was this girl,'*" Freddy began in his understated Norwegian accent. "I followed Ash up here to PSB about a year or so later, as a replacement for an injured dancer, after my . . ." He shook his head. "Well, let's say that being in Capitol City had lost its charm. I see it now as a classic relocation cure. Anyway, a couple years in, I meet this girl at a meet and greet. She was exotic, brilliant, and liked to drink as much as I did. A match made in hell, as it turned out.

"By then I was starting to have a nip in the mornings. She starts talking about retirement and 401k's, houses, insurance, and so forth, and what was my plan when it was time to stop dancing. Stuff I never even thought about. She was a database administrator, and pushed—well, she encouraged me in the technology direction, as well."

He glanced around the table, and Zoe, not for one moment, turned away.

"I started to study on my own. A lot of tech positions don't require a college degree but have their own certifications. I wasn't as technically proficient as she, and the work largely bored me. But I was pretty competent and a bit of a charmer, so it wasn't too difficult to land a project management job at Amalgam Inc.

"Over time, and with the newness having worn off, I began to get more and more depressed. I indulged my alcoholism and started dabbling in cocaine—which allowed me to drink more."

"Why were you depressed, Freddy?" Zoe asked.

"Other than all the alcohol and coke, you mean?" said Freddy, laughing.

Zoe just smiled and waited. I noticed she was being especially attentive, as if all her mothering instinct was now homed in on Freddy.

"I never wanted an office job growing up, it sounded like death to me. I missed my crazy artsy friends."

"Didn't you make friends where you worked?" I asked.

"I did, but—in the corporate world—it's just different. Outside of sports, I found it hard to relate. Great people, but quite frankly, folks who wouldn't know the difference between a waltz and a polonaise—"

"Or a mazurka," intoned Zoe.

"Exactly! Thank you, Bell," Freddy, still holding Zoe's hands, took a moment to kiss them before continuing.

"People who never listened to Villa Lobos or Prokofiev, let alone went to the ballet or saw plays. Folks who had never even heard of Nijinsky and thought the art of Thomas Kinkade the very height of sophistication."

"Ouch!" said Ash.

"Okay," Freddy continued, "that's a little unfair, and I do realise I'm coming off as a conceited ass—not to mention Kathryn told me so—that was her name, by the way. But these things are important to me! So, I tried to focus on sports, and usually this involved drinking. Sports, alcohol, and cocaine became my life, but I was trying to make it work."

"But Ash was up here," I said, "and other folks from PSB. Couldn't you have—"

"On the one hand I knew I was becoming a bit of a mess, and I wanted to hide that from my dance friends. And on the other, Kathryn was jealous of the time I spent with my people without her. And if she did come, she'd complain she felt left out. In addition, I found it difficult myself. Like I was an outsider looking in, but no longer really a part of it. And it all happened very fast. From dancing professionally to getting a job in the tech industry was maybe a year—no adjustment period."

He continued, "Kathryn had her own love of drink, and what started out as pleasant night on the town often ended in inebriated sex or drunken rows—often both. She had a larger salary than I did, and she thought I was riding her coattails for the money."

"Eventually," Freddy shook his head, "she met this actor at an after-show event. I won't go into details but, poor slob—I can't help but wonder if he isn't enrolled in computer school now," he laughed. "It's as if she's drawn to creative types, then tries to beat the spirit right out of them until she gets bored with their newfound domesticity and needs a new project."

"Are you still angry?" I asked.

Freddy took a moment to consider. "At the time I was furious! I'm sure I ran around the grief bases several times.

My drinking and coke habit went off the charts, and I started missing a lot of work."

"What was the lure of drinking?" asked Ash.

"Loneliness—that is, anything that would make it go away—my feeling of isolation. See—no matter how awful I was feeling, I knew if I just drank enough, there would be this moment where everything would be all right. It was an illusion, of course, as I'd just wake up to the same problems from the day before. And of course, there's a big genetic factor."

"Did your parents drink?" asked Zoe.

"It depends what you mean by 'drink.' I saw my dad tie one on a few times at big gatherings, but this was very much the exception. I never saw him drunk outside of those events. That being said, I know both of his brothers had issues. Uncle Jan got sober when I was around eleven, but Uncle Karl died of exposure on a hunting trip. He was found sitting on the ground leaning up against a tree, a rifle in his lap and still holding his bottle. According to the autopsy, he was both well under the influence and well over the limit, so there is no doubt alcohol was a contributing factor. I never saw my mother more than slightly tipsy, and even that was pretty rare."

"Go on, Freddy, we're listening," Zoe said.

"Once Kathryn took off, I realised I had lost everything. As odd as it sounds, she was my tether. She was the one thing I still had tying me to my old life. Once she left, I found myself in a world so bleak, that frankly, I just didn't care anymore. I had no friends, no art, no dance . . . no relationship. I had a type of job that was the very epitome of what I had dreaded as a child."

Freddy paused and looked out at the Sound for a weighted moment before continuing.

"To make a long story short, I got so piss-drunk and coked up one night, trying to find that moment—that relief, but this time, it didn't seem to help . . ."

He paused again, looking blankly at the table before continuing.

"So I grabbed a tie and hung myself in the closet."

"Freddy!?" Zoe exclaimed. I noticed her big brown eyes were welling up, as were my own. Apparently unaware of this detail, Ash too looked grave.

"Look—after a couple minutes the dowel broke and I regained consciousness. I called a friend from work, and with her help, checked myself into rehab."

"I packaged that up rather nicely for you, but in reality, it wasn't quite that neat."

"Freddy, we had no idea!" said Zoe, tears flowing unashamedly from her eyes.

"Really, I'm better now. Much better. A little fat still, I turned to ice cream out of rehab, but I'm working on losing that as well."

"Do you have a higher power?" asked Ash.

"Ash!" I said, smacking him on the arm. I thought he was making a joke, but seeing his face, I saw he was serious. He took my smacking hand and held it, turning to me with a glance, letting me know he meant no such thing.

"Yeah!" Freddy said. "For me it was 'being in the zone.' You know when you're dancing or doing sports and it all just comes together? Like when you're performing better than ever, but at the same time—you're not the one doing it."

Hearing that surprises me. My head jerks up, and I immediately think back to that day spent rehearsing the tango with Ash.

"So anyway, I just sort of try to be open to that . . . presence in the rest of my life." He pauses. "Listen, our food is getting cold, but I felt like I owed it to you guys, you know—the truth. A little honesty for a change. I realise that has not always been my policy."

At his last words, my head again involuntarily jerks slightly, and just for a moment my compartmentalisation falters; as Saturday looms closer and the spectre of Marcus and what I must do draws near.

"Stef?" I return to the room to find Freddy looking at me. "Are you all right?" he asks.

"Of course!" I exclaim "I'm fine—*I'm always fine!*" I say in my perky best.

Freddy chuckles and bites his lip. Ash puts his hands to his face to hide a laugh, and even Zoe can't stop herself from smiling.

I feel exposed—a complete imposter.

"Excuse me!" I yell to our waitress, flustered, *"can we get some more coffee?"*

34
Little Stefanie

Serafina was passed to Ash, then me, then Freddy, who was reluctant to give her up.

"I spilled my guts," said Freddy. "I think it's your turn, Zoe. Where did this little angel come from?"

"From God, of course." Zoe smiled sweetly.

"See, Stef?" Ash said. "I told you it was immaculate conception."

"Well," continued Zoe, "if you must know . . ."

Zoe glanced around the room, then leaned forward so other tables wouldn't be able to hear. She began quietly, seriously, and looked at us intently as she spoke.

"As you know, I've been saving the semen of the men I have 'been with' in the freezer for the last six or seven years. Rating them on their sexual prowess and labelling them with dates and times—it's more cost effective that way—than using a bank, that is."

Freddy and I started laughing immediately, but my poor Ash, face frozen, soon saw he had been taken in by the joke.

"Oh, come on, Ash!" Zoe exclaimed. "Seriously!? That was way too easy. The truth is pretty simple. I wanted a baby, I was on a holiday, I found an attractive man, a surfer—why not? And now I have one—no strings attached."

"Of course," she continued, "if you want something saucier, I have a story about a monk who wouldn't sleep with me unless I could recite verbatim any passage from the New Testament. Guess who won that?"

Zoe had matured too. I don't think I'd realised it, as we were in such close contact until she went home for a year. She was still Zoe, but more reflective. She had a keenness in her eyes, a knowingness I'd never sensed before.

35
Ridicule

The following morning, picking up some caffeine along the way, we head to the studio. It was the only full day the four of us could spend together before I had to fly home in order to . . . "conclude things."

In order to keep the dread at bay, and not wanting to miss a second of our reunion, I intended to keep my mind productively engaged in every moment.

Freddy and Zoe used to perform a wonderful one-armed ice-skating lift where the woman ends up being supported above the man's head by his hand at her hip. She's on her side, horizontal in the air, and the pair of them are spinning. They had promised to teach it to us years ago, but we had simply never gotten around to it.

Freddy and Zoe first demonstrated the lift. Despite a few extra pounds on both their parts, Zoe being a new mum, and the fact they hadn't partnered with each other for six years, they performed it beautifully.

"Okay, guys, it's your turn," Zoe coached. "From the preparation, Stevie, your left hand is going on Ash's shoulder. You'll need to battement your left leg almost sideways, leaning into him as he takes your weight. His right hand will plant on your hip, and his left will be on the knee of your throwing leg."

"Ash," Freddy continued, "when Stef throws her leg, you'll need to try lift her up in one go and immediately start spinning clockwise. Then release your hand on her leg so you're supporting her only with your right. It's a little counter-intuitive at first, as you will be spinning in the opposite direction of her momentum."

"Christ!" said Ash, coming to terms with the physical mechanics involved. "Why not just dress up a 150-pound dumbbell in a tutu? It would be a lot less hassle."

"Hey!" I protested. "Closer to a hundred is more like! And Freddy managed with Zoe no problem."

Ash was both a few inches taller than Freddy and outweighed him by about 25 pounds. While before her pregnancy, Zoe and I had nearly always been exactly the same height and weight—she might have had a couple of pounds on me. "It's the boobs," she would joke.

"Come on, Ash, give it a go," said Freddy, ignoring us. "Stefanie, are you ready?"

"I'm sorry," I said, still provoked—and at the same time— unable to resist . . .

"Ash usually needs at least a couple of 'go's' to get me ready." I suppress a grin.

"Ohh . . ." countered Ash. He turned to me and placed his hands on his hips—taking up the challenge. "I see how it is. I thought that after all this time, I finally got my Stefanie, but it turns out all I really got was a 'Stef infection.'" Ash grinned mischievously.

Game on!

Admittedly, Ash's remark was rather clever, but under no circumstances was I going to let him know that.

"Hmmm . . . 'Stef infection,' brilliant," I repeated with a decided lack of enthusiasm, while simultaneously, my mechanism began its churn.

"Tell me, Ash, was that a spur-of-the-moment improvisation? Or did you think of it years ago, write it down, and just kept it folded in your pocket all this time, waiting for your moment?"

A nod to Jane Austen. Apparently innumerable sleepless nights listening to *Pride and Prejudice* had not been in vain.

"It's called having a verbal advantage, sweetheart, and mine's growing all the time," said Ash.

"Growing all the time!?" I shake my head, acting confused. "Oh! Are we still talking about your vocabulary?"

"You know, Stef—fa—nie," said Ash, ignoring the bait, "I could start calling you 'Fanny' instead of 'Stef'—as in 'Ash couldn't complete the lift due to the size of her enormous fanny!'"

Zoe gasped and covered her mouth in surprise. Her eyes grew wide while my own reduced to slits.

An American through and through, Ash's remark was cruder than he likely realised. 'Fanny' having distinctly other associations outside the States. But knowing both his intention and dialectal naiveté, I plowed ahead. Indeed, it was but fuel for my fire—and today, I fully intended to feast on Roast Ash.

Connections began blazing through my brain: dialect-fire-burn-Ash-arse . . . Hmmmm.

"Here's an interesting fact, Monsieur Soulier," I retort.

"Did you know that in French your nickname wouldn't be 'Ash' but 'Ass'? As in, 'Oh Seb-*ASS*-tien—Oh that's right, *j'ai oublié, tu parles pas français*." (I forgot, you don't speak French.)

"My American 'ass' was good enough for you last night."

I cross my arms and turn my head in mock abhorrence. "'Arse,' Sebastian, please," I say in my most peevish accent. "Stop desecrating the Queen's English with your vulgar Americanisms."

"Oh, woman!" Ash says, shaking his head and sporting a twisted grin, "you are so cruising for a bruising!" He draws nearer and starts to reach for me.

His somewhat canned response tells me he's already beginning to falter.

My mind shifts into fifth, all pistons firing—but I'm not going to give it away, either. After all, a tepid jab deserves a tepid response. That's a quote from *The Art of War*—and if it's not, it ought to be.

"Fair warning, Sebastian," I say, feigning boredom with a

yawn. "Playing with fire is a fools' errand—and a firestorm from me will reduce you to—*Ash!*" Then I smirk, back away, and maintain the distance.

There's no need to outwit him—after all, he'll get himself plenty tangled if I just keep handing him rope.

"It's really up to you, Stefanie," says Ash, continuing his approach. "You can either go up in this lift—or, woman, *you are going to go down!*"

And there it is!

"Go down!?" I ask, my tone rising incredulously. "Is that some sort of metaphor? *Or just more talk and no action?*"

Ash simply glares at me; I see his mental gears turning. An *"I was afraid I'd get Stef infection"* jab would have been perfect here, and he knows it, but he's already given that one away, and in a verbal joust, timing is everything.

"Cat got your tongue, Ash? Flipping through your 'rolodexia de retortium,' but coming up empty?"

With squinted eyes and twisted lips, Ash searches his mind for something to volley back over the net at me. It's on the tip of his tongue—the runway lights are flashing—but he just can't seem to land it.

"Tell me, Ash, shall I deliver the 'coup de grâce' in English, or in another language you don't speak?"

Ash bunches up his face and squints at me—but still has nothing.

With Ash on the ropes, I go for a knockout. I walk

determinedly over to the piano, atop of which is a pen and notepad—

"If you fancy keeping notes in your pocket," I say, handing him the pad, "write this down." As Sebastian automatically begins to reach for it, I impatiently snatch it back. *"Here,* I'll do it for you."

I speak the words slowly as I scribble them down in haste: *"Always remember Sebastian (comma) Never bring a hen to a cockfight."*

Admittedly, less of an 'olive branch' and more of a 'poke in the eye with a sharp stick,' I tear off the page and hold it out for him to take while I stare at him blankly.

This time he expends no effort to receive my offering, in fact, stone faced and glaring at me, my poor Ash seems to have entirely lost the plot.

"Of course, you can always just google it," I say, now crumpling up the note in my hand. "Just go to Stefanies-Sarcastic-Slights.com—we're offering a thirty percent discount for the rhetorically challenged and those whose intellectual pretensions unfailingly betray them to place . . . how does one say it . . . left of centre?"

And with that, I toss the crumpled paper ball over to Ash. It sails in a big arc, and making no attempt to catch it, bounces off the top of Ash's head.

I stand my ground and cross my arms. "My, my," I say slowly, shaking my head with disappointment. "How are the mighty fallen . . ." Daring him.

Brimming with tension, for a moment Ash stands motionless, then without warning—*he pounces.*

Giddy and shrieking, I evade capture by running figure eights around Freddy and Zoe. Ash chases me about the studio until I spy the sofa in the foyer and decide that it's an immensely suitable place to be tackled.

Tackling turns to tickling, and tickling becomes touching. My back on the sofa, Ash on top of me, I wrap my legs behind his back, and he lifts me until he is standing. My legs around his waist, my arms embracing his head. We are in mid snog when—

"Ahem, I'm sorry, Bell," Freddy asks. "What did you say?"

"I said, I think it's a good time to crack open a new novel," said Zoe.

Ash and I freeze in mid-passion. Our cheeks are pressed together, as we have turned our heads to face them. I slide down Ash's trunk like a fireman's pole, accidentally taking down his sweatpants in the process, until my bottom hits the ground.

"Really, Stefanie!" says Ash, hands on hips and grinning down at me. "If I'd known you were that determined to get into my pants, I'd have scheduled you an appointment."

I have a retort ready. Something along the lines of *"Why bother with an appointment when your calendar is obviously wide open?"* but it occurs to me, not for the first time this week, that I'm in love with this man—this kind and caring creature, and with a mischievous smile, I allow him the last word.

And how so very different are my interactions with Marcus.

153

36
The Enigma of Freddy

That evening, while dining at Palomino and discussing plans, still intrigued by Freddy's story at lunch, I was now curious to know more.

"Freddy, do you mind me asking? You never said—back at CCB, how did you . . . Why did you?—"

"I want to know too!" said Zoe.

"Ahh," he said, "I sort of skipped that part. You want the condensed version?"

"I want the bucket of popcorn version!" exclaimed Zoe.

Freddy shook his head, rubbed his forehead, and drew his hand down over his face, gathering his thoughts. "I was a bit of a chubby kid and small, and if you can believe it, quite shy. Sort of like Ash is now," he teased.

"Oh god, not another one," groaned Ash.

"It turns out, my brothers and sisters were all chubby until puberty, when they all sort of magically transformed, but being the youngest by several years, I didn't know that, and no one bothered to tell me."

He continued, "Dancing was a way of expressing myself in a way I couldn't do verbally. And like my siblings, I lost the flab when I sprouted up."

"This is all very interesting, Freddy," said Zoe, "but get to the good part."

With her elbows on the table, Zoe placed her head in her hands and gazed at him, blinking her eyes, rapt with attention.

"A little patience, Zolitia!" Freddy countered. "Popcorn takes time to pop."

"Around the age of thirteen," he continued, "I was noticed by Julian Halvorsen, a new teacher at our school. He was young, maybe early thirties, about my age now actually. I don't know why he wasn't still dancing himself. I asked once, but never received an answer that satisfied. Now, I think I have a better idea."

"Anyway, he was brilliant, articulate, worldly, and really everything I wanted to be in life. He took a shine to me early on and took me under his wing. I looked to him for guidance and he became my mentor."

"I was starting to lose the flab, but still had a chubby kid mentality, and still very shy—especially with girls who were beginning to attract my attention at this point. I'm maybe fourteen now."

"His instruction went far beyond ballet. We discussed

philosophy, and frequented museums. I learned about music and art, he was no fan of Balanchine either by the way."

"A wise man indeed," said Ash.

"Feeling graced by allowing me into his confidence, we talked about anything and everything." Freddy continued. "And he was such a charmer."

"I confessed to being too afraid to really talk to girls. And he wisely, gave me some insight into their minds."

"Julian liked his wine—'for the tannins'—he would say. And he let me drink as well. Though at first, it was just a glass of wine with dinner, the gesture itself made me feel like an adult and it had the effect of really loosening me up."

"As time went on, more and more I would spend weekends with him and the occasional night on the sofa. This was no issue with my parents. I was a good kid and he was a very respected instructor at the school and as I've said, charming. In fact, he could charm the pants off of anyone, and late one night with more than a few glasses of wine in me . . . he did. I was fifteen years old."

Freddy paused, reflecting, and he seemed to gaze into nothing for a moment.

"Leading up to this, he had told me that women might have the 'facilities,' as he put it, meaning sexually, to satisfy me, but that it would be wrong to limit myself, and that if I found a man whom I loved, then I should love that man wholeheartedly."

"In hindsight . . ." he paused, "I can see where, via his charm, and worldly knowledge, I surrendered some of my critical facility. Where at first I would challenge him and his ideas, he would have such a compelling argument in the other direction that eventually, though his ideas were at times bizarre, I just assumed what he said must be the truth."

"Such as . . .?" I asked.

"Well, for instance, he told me once that no matter what, women always feel guilty about sex—that it's filthy."

Zoe and I just looked at each other for a moment then chuckled.

"Yeah, well everyone knows guilty sex is the best!" laughed Zoe.

"Zóza!?—Why you filthy little bitch!" I teased, and we all laughed.

"You have to understand, I did love Julian, and I still think of him as my mentor. And at that point, I had never been with a girl—too shy to make an approach, too fearful of rejection.

"Now all of a sudden, here is a person making an approach on me, giving me the attention I had so wanted from girls. And he was someone I had the utmost respect and faith in. And having at that point no experience to the contrary, and very much under his influence, well—and of course, I was very much inebriated.

"Our relationship continued for another year or so until I got picked up by a touring company. But even prior to this occurring, I began to see the occasional slip in his personality. From being confidant and charming one moment he would descend into acting like an insolent child—selfish and extremely needy. It was very disconcerting, to say the least.

"I don't know if it was intentional, but the impact it had on me—well, I became very dependent on staying in his good graces, which meant insofar as possible, keeping his mood elevated."

"Can you say that again?" asked Ash.

"Look, I don't want overstate this, but if someone you respect and admire shines their light on you, it's as if you're the only person in their world. If they then suddenly withdraw that attention, that love, it can have a devastating effect. You'll do almost anything to get it back.

"And I think on some level he knew this. No—with everything he knew about how people worked, how to play with their emotions and desires, I'm sure he knew this, and he used it in a small way to control me . . . I don't think I've ever said that out loud before."

"Anyway," Freddy tosses off the unexpected emotional weight of it and continues.

"Like I was saying, I was with a touring company for my first couple of years. I'm sixteen or seventeen now and girls were starting to notice me. And there was one in the company who was, well, we shall say she was more aggressive than the rest.

"She was from Iceland and a couple of years older than me. Confidant and gregarious. And late one night, pleasantly drunk in her hotel room, she asked me about my training

in Norway. And I spoke about Julian, some of which I
just related.

"Then she point-blank asked me if we had a sexual relationship. I confided that we had. She asked me if I was gay, and
honestly I don't remember answering.

"'So, Freddy," she asked, 'have you ever been with a girl?'
All I remember is that I was frozen, and my heart was racing.
Then she placed her hand on the back of my head, drew me
in, and kissed me."

Freddy fell silent and seemed to have reached the end of
his story.

"And!?" Zoe said impatiently.

"And . . . the pizza arrived, we stuffed our faces, and passed
out watching *The Matrix*."

"Ohhh, Freddy don't be cruel!" pleaded Zoe.

"Listen, despite all my transgressions, one thing Julian taught
me was discretion. And even back in my drinking days, I've
never been a bragger of exploits—*not that I haven't had any!*

"Now it's true he might have been worried about protect-
ing our little secret. But he thought—and I agree—that it's
the epitome of classlessness to 'kiss and tell' and a little
unseemly to brag to one's friends."

"So, you're a bagger, but not a bragger?" I teased.

"Freddy, the gentleman bagger?" embellished Ash.

"Do you want me to continue or not?"

We all shut up immediately.

Freddy opened his mouth, but no words emerged. Then he gestured with his hands and finally managed, "In any case, we spent much of the remainder of the tour—"

"Shagging?" asked Zoe.

Freddy pursed his lips and raised his brows but said nothing further.

"Did you ever see Julian again?" I asked.

Freddy looked down suddenly a little sad, then nodded. "Yes, a couple of years later. He was decidedly worse. By that time the alcohol was always a presence. And no—as I'm sure you're all curious—we didn't.

"I was surprised at how upset he became. Upset, angry, and belligerent. He wanted to fall into old patterns, but I had moved on so to speak. Cracks in his facade I had only glimpsed before were now becoming obvious.

"I know a lot of this was the drinking, and though I could see it in him, I couldn't see it was beginning to impact my own life as well. And anyway, even if I had been gay, by that time he was often sloppily unattractive.

"A few years later, I received word that he had died. The way it was put was that he killed himself, which I always took to mean suicide. He OD'd on painkillers.

"Now I'm no longer sure if it was intentional or not. He had been fired, and I don't know but can guess some of the details. Even while I was still there, he started taking an interest in other students."

"Did that make you jealous?" asked Zoe.

Freddy took some time to consider. "No, although I don't doubt it was part of his game. Another string to pull, another way to manipulate Freddy the puppet.

"Actually, by that time, having lived a little, I was relived and excited to get the hell out of there again—get on with my life. Also, for what it's worth, and despite my other issues, I seem to have been given a free pass in the jealousy department."

"Come again?" I asked.

"I can get depressed, and I can get angry, but I think I've only been jealous maybe exactly one time for an hour or so, I can actually pinpoint the day."

"You're kidding," said Ash.

"I mean jealous in that bitter vindictive, righteous indigna-tion sort of way. I can get envious, of course—say of Bell's attitude turns, or Ash's . . ." Freddy thought for a moment. "Come to think of it—Ash isn't particularly enviable."

We laughed, and it lightened up the mood.

"Humph," Ash snorted.

"But envy, in the way I mean it, doesn't carry the same emotional weight."

37
Gimme Three Steps

"So, you don't consider yourself bi or gay?" intoned Zoe.

She was sitting in the booth next to Freddy, and the way she posed the question, her inflection, and the way she tossed her hair when she asked I found most intriguing.

"No, Bell, I consider myself straight. Open-minded, but straight. My mother used to say as a kid I was a good eater. I'd try anything once and usually twice, even if I didn't like it the first time, just to be sure."

"Sooo," Zoe spurred him on, "what happened at CCB?"

Freddy shook his head, "I can't give you a definitive answer. I didn't do it before or after CCB, nor with anyone I saw outside the company. And it wasn't planned—the first time, anyway. I guess part of it was it worked, and I have to say, it worked very well.

"And, I found it extremely amusing, like I had this secret identity. And lastly, well, I never said I was gay, but somehow it was assumed, and I didn't bother to correct it."

"Enough with the philosophy, Freddy!" I implored.

"We want details!" added Zoe.

"Okay! Jesus—I'm getting there. Ash, do you get interrogated like this?"

Ash shook his head. "I don't have such a colourful history . . . unfortunately."

"First of all, by the time I came to CCB, it was six or seven years later. I'm in my mid-twenties by now. I had matured and had tested the waters enough to have grown quite, well, confidant."

At this point, Zoe made a big display of arching her back, stretching her arms over her head and yawning.

"Oh for Pete's sake, alright!" Freddy exclaimed, but he was unable to keep from chuckling at Zoe's antics himself.

"How it started was, late one night one of the dancers, who shall remain nameless, and I were speaking in her flat at an after party shortly after I—"

"Was it Mira?" I interrupted?

"Kyla," Zoe said confidently. "Sorry, Freddy, we're just trying to get a little context." She smiled innocently.

"Shortly after I arrived at CCB," continued Freddy, ignoring us. "She was nice, but not being particularly flirty, and I wasn't sure what to make of that. But then she asked me to come talk in her room, where it was quieter. Naturally, I assumed she was up for a little midnight mischief.

"And in her room, she did start undressing, but really casually, and then only to change into some sweats. She was completely relaxed about it, and continued our conversation the whole time, almost like I wasn't there.

"And again, I wasn't sure what to think. I mean, on the one hand, we are dancers after all, and maybe she was just a little more immodest than the rest of us."

Among other things, Freddy referenced the numerous quick changes—that is, backstage costume changes—one had to do during a performance. Often there was no time run to the dressing room, and one simply had to make do with the cover of helpers in the wings.

"I'm sure at some point, everyone at CCB has seen me naked," I agreed.

The three of them started chuckling—but, as we've all been there—a little more than I thought it warranted.

"Ahem," Freddy said, gesturing with his eyes.

I glanced back, only to find our waiter had been standing just behind me the whole time. "CCB?," he asks "is that Chuck's Construction and Bedrock?"

The three of them begin to laugh heartily at my expense.

The waiter pours me some more wine, "This glass is on me dear—I think you're going need it."

"It's okay" Zoe explained to the waiter, "we're artists."

Satisfied and suppressing a smile, the waiter nodded, did a military about-face, and marched away from our table.

"Don't worry, Stevie, he gets it," Zóza continued. "He's probably an actor."

I'm relieved when Freddy picks up where he left off.

"Anyway, when she finished changing and sat back down on the on the bed, still chatting away, I was actually thinking *she* was a lesbian.

"And then out of nowhere she asks me, 'Freddy, have you ever been with a girl?' Practically the same words as Miss Iceland all those years ago. And I thought to myself *'Oh fuck!'*, and I finally understood what was happening.

"To be honest, I felt a little insulted, but then the thought occurred . . . And me, being the dishonourable dog that I was, and so as not to embarrass her—at least that was my rationalisation at the time—I decided to, well, play along.

"And so it began. And by the way, don't think that other girls in the company didn't know about me getting around. In fact, I'm sure of it. *Girls talk too.* So if they considered me a friend with benefits or a late night go-to, it was fine by me."

I tried not to smirk as names such as "Ready Freddy" and "Shag-Buddy Danielsson" readily sprang to mind; then I looked up to see Zoe's keen brown eyes looking directly at me.

She crinkled her nose ever so slightly—gave me the subtlest of squints—and I decided to keep my mouth shut.

Honestly, every so often I wonder if Zóza can read my thoughts.

"In the end I figured," Freddy shrugged, "if the girls had decided it was their group mission in life to 'turn me' or 'straighten me out' . . . *why not let them turn and straighten me as often as possible?"*

"Oh my god!" exclaimed Ash, bringing his hands to his head. *"You're my fucking hero!"*

We all laughed, but Freddy continued. "Ash, it was fun while it lasted, but it didn't last."

"Well, don't stop now," said Zoe. "What happened!?"

"By this time, you had all left CCB, when a brash young queen named Javier joined the company. Javier was loud and proud, hotblooded, and extremely opinionated.

"And I'm not just being a dick. Everyone thought that. He wasn't a bad-looking guy, but there was something about him, something in his personality that was extremely off-putting. Richie especially didn't care for him. He said one's sexual preference shouldn't be your single defining feature."

"What do you mean?" I asked.

"Rich put it like this. He said, 'look, I'm an artist, a dancer, I'm politically savvy, like to cook, and I'm studying to be an architect . . . and I also "happen" to be gay. Javier, on the other hand—I think dancing is just a hobby for him. *Being gay is his real occupation*.'"

"I tend to agree—you don't see straight men acting this way," said Ash.

"That's not true," I said. "What about that night at Hamburger Mary's? Those two seemed rather hyper-masculine to me."

Ash pursed his lips and thought for a moment. "Touché," he conceded.

"Well, look at you," I teased, "and here I thought you didn't speak French."

Ash puts on his best smoulder and, in a French accent, says, "It's true, I possess a certain *'je ne sais quoi—non?'*

"No," we all said simultaneously.

"I hear you and Zoe went all MMA on them," said Ash, ignoring us. "I wish I'd have seen it. I came two seconds too late."

"I don't like to think about it, Ash," said Freddy soberly. "I still have a lot of shame around that incident. I had been drinking. I wasn't drunk, but I certainly had a good buzz going. I keep thinking how it could have gone differently. And later I found out that in addition to a smashed nose, the big one had to have reconstructive dental surgery."

"Freddy!" countered Zoe. "Stop it! I don't know what we would have done if you weren't there."

"It appears you can handle yourself, Bell."

"Well, I couldn't," I piped in. "What could I have done? Rond de jame'd him in *zijn ballen*!?"

Ash and Freddy looked at me, not understanding.

"You know," I tried again. "Bollocks—"

"Balls!" exclaimed Zoe, coming to my rescue.

"Freddy, I don't want you remembering it any other way,"

Zóza implored. "It's too bad about 'Little John,' but Stevie and I are still here—and unscathed."

"You mentioned PTSD on the way out, Freddy. What was that about?"

"Can we save that one for another time, Stef? Shouldn't I finish the one story before starting another?"

"Yes, please," said Zoe.

"Do continue," I agreed.

"Okay, back to Javier." Freddy took a breath and collected his thoughts. "You remember Rich and Enrico were a couple? Well, one night when we were all having some drinks down at Mary's, they started complaining that Javier had been incessantly, blatantly propositioning them."

"First he went after Richie, who flat-out turned him down. Then he immediately went to Enrico, who likewise told him to get lost. Then he tried to get them to have a three-way. And the way he went about it lacked any subtlety—"

"I've forgotten," Zoe laughed. "What exactly is the politically correct way to suggest a three-way these days?"

"I'm just saying he was relentless, and needlessly crude. Anyway, when that didn't happen . . . *Guess who was next on his list?*"

"Uh-oh," said Ash.

"Yeah!" said Freddy. "And this all takes place in the first two or three weeks he is there. So when I likewise turn him down, *he is pissed!*"

"Another show, another party, and another rejection for Javier. And this time from none other than 'Vinnie Vaginitis.'"

"Not old 'who's afraid to smell Vincent Wolfe?'" asked Ash.

"Yeah, of all people, so you know he was getting desperate. When out of nowhere, I hear Javier exclaim from across the room, *'What's wrong with all you people!?'"* Freddy imperson- ated. *"'I guess no one likes to fuck around here!'*

"Seriously, that's what he was like. And then, immediately following that little chestnut, he blasted out, *'And I don't think Freddy's even gay—all he does is sleep with girls.'*

"Now, I don't know how he figured it out, who he spoke to, or if he actually even did. Knowing Javier, he might very well have just been bitching. But nevertheless, that seed took root and began to spread, and it spread fast."

"I spent a good three weeks of living in my own private hell of 'women scorned' before Ash called and said a spot had opened up at PSB. I picked up my shit and I and left. End of story."

"And the end of an era," Ash mused.

"Wait a minute," I said, trying to work it out. "You're saying the girls didn't seem to mind you getting around as long as they thought you were gay, but when they found out you weren't. . ." Not wanting to make assumptions, I finished with gestures.

Freddy and Ash just glanced at each other, collectively shook their heads, and together said: *"Women!"*

"Enough about me!" said Freddy. *"Zoe!* What's your infamous backstory? Full of tawdry, licentious croc hunters in the outback, I hope?"

Zoe crinkled up her nose and squinted. "Sheep—mostly a lot of sheep."

"I believe you, Zoe," said Freddy, though not sounding especially convinced.

"Though—when I was fourteen," Zoe volunteered, "I did take a fancy to a young Joey—"

"And?" inquired Freddy.

"Turned out he was a bit of a mama's boy—every time I made an approach he went and jumped in his mother's pouch."

Freddy rolled his eyes. After having just been given the third degree, he was hardly content to let Zoe's answer rest at that, when Sebastian's phone rang.

38
Disillusion

"Hello? Yes, we have the old crew together—just finished rehearsing."

"And she's saved by the 'bell'—unbelievable!" exclaimed Freddy.

Zoe smiled sweetly, inclined her head to the side, and tapped lightly on her cheek, indicating where Freddy should kiss her.

"That's all you get for now," she said as Freddy acquiesced.

An intriguing double entendre of her own? I muse.

"Sure . . ." Sebastian says, still focused on his call.
Sebastian's demeanour takes a serious turn as he listens.

Whomever is on the other end goes on for a while; Zoe and Freddy sense it too. Our side talk dies down as we try and glean details from Ash's side of the conversation.

"I see . . . No, I appreciate it—I know you did your best . . . Well, a bit . . . I guess it would have really given us some breathing space . . . Yeah, sure. Maybe next week. Sounds good . . . Thanks, John, for letting me know."

Ash disconnects and puts the phone on the table.

"Ash?" says Freddy.

"That was John from the Arts Commission. He just called to let me know in advance that if it's going to happen with the grant at all—it's definitely *not* going to happen this year.

"We're not established enough, or don't have enough street cred, or . . . Listen, we're not dead in the water, and nothing currently on the calendar is cancelled. It was probably too soon, anyway. I mean, it was for Hilarion. Honestly, I'm relieved in a way—really."

Ash tries to spin it light, but I can feel his disappointment.

* * *

We stayed out too late that night with Zoe and Freddy. Trying to make light of the bitter grant disappointment, we danced, laughed, reminisced, and spoke of better things to come.

"Please, guys, don't not drink on account of me," said Freddy.

"Nothing for me, I'm still nursing," said Zoe.

Ash nursed a couple of beers all night. And I, never much of a drinker, but wanting to block out tomorrow's ordeal with Marcus as effectively as possible, managed to sneak a couple Jäger shots at the bar while picking up drinks for Ash and me. Maybe it was three—*maybe I lost count.*

They indulged me a bit as I didn't want it to end, but eventually, Zoe had to get back to Serafina.

Becoming more sozzled than I intended, I remember Ash

waking me up in the taxi (or was it an Uber?) outside his flat, helping me up the stairs, and putting me to bed.

Second Variation

39
It Comes in Threes

I find myself in the middle of a barren road. To my left, the bridge is collapsing in ruins. Metal whines as it bends. Concrete cracks and falls in blocks, disintegrating into the blackness below. Dust obfuscates my view, and I can no longer see Ash.

In front of me, the convertible lurches at me a few inches at a time. Its enormous engine bellows in my ear, challenging me. Its redness has darkened to colour of blood. Unable to move, I hear Ash's voice calling for me. I search, but I can't find him. Suddenly, I hear the shriek of tires on pavement and turn back to see it, no longer only a car, a metal thing, but a presence, accelerating towards me.

40
Agitation

Saturday, December 21st

"Stef?"

I sleep poorly and awake more than slightly hungover. The previous night's escapades are hazy now, no more than a distant memory; it's only the dream that lingers.

On edge and distracted, I begin the day smoking cigarettes, drinking coffee, and I never really stop. I barely notice the cloud of smoke forming in the kitchen.

After a while, Ash turns on the ventilation fan without comment.

Taking only a few items with me, there was nothing to do but wait. I pace about, then realising that I'm pacing, go to the bathroom to check my makeup, check my hair.

I sit for a moment, but I'm up again the next second, to check my purse, or to see if I need to pack anything further. I check the clock repeatedly. Check, check, check. And still an hour and thirty-seven minutes until it was time to leave the flat.

"I can take you to the airport if you want."

I hear Ash's voice, but it doesn't register.

"Hmmm?" I say, looking up.

"Stefanie, are you okay?"

"Yes! . . . It's just pre-flight jitters." I smile thinly and light another cigarette, only to find I have one already burning in the ashtray.

In truth, I was not okay. I'd spent my entire life avoiding confrontation—avoiding Mother. And to that end, I would take whatever means necessary. I loved her, yet in that moment, I loathed her—yet still envied her strength, her resolve.

My mind raced ceaselessly for an alternative to the confrontation with Marcus. An escape plan, a loophole in the dubious clause. My skin was crawling. My insides felt hollow, stretched and full of wasps. And I hadn't even reached the airport.

Absentmindedly, I reach for my coffee and knock it off the table. As it hits the floor, china shatters, and coffee goes everywhere; an alarmed Jasper leaps up and scatters across the floor.

"Godverdomme!" I stand up, *"Kut, Kut, Kanker!"* One hand goes to my head, the other is clenched in a fist. I feel my nails digging into the palm of my hand and clench even harder. I realise I'm visibly shaking.

"Stefanie!?" Ash is over immediately. He tries to console me, but he may as well console an angry rock; it would be less frigid. I remember Freddy's story from lunch and wonder if Ash has a tie lying about.

Stop it!

But my mind can't sit still. In Sebastian's full embrace, I resign myself to sit again.

"I'll come with you, Stefanie."

"You can't. We spent everything on Zoe's ticket, and you have . . ." I shake my head. I can't find the words for "classes and rehearsals," and it doesn't matter anyway. I glance up to see Ash is suffering, seeing me like this, and for a moment, I'm able to get out of myself.

"Thank you, though," I say, touching his face.

Ash sits on the sofa next to me. With his left arm around my shoulders, he places his right hand on my tummy like he used to do when I was nervous before a performance, just before going on stage.

"Breathe, Stefanie."

Through the fabric of my blouse, I feel the light press of his hand upon my abdomen. I close my eyes and breathe. I focus on the pressure of his hand on my tummy. Breathing in against his palm, feeling the tender resistance, the gentle warmth . . . breathing out, the soft pressure . . . breathing . . . breathing . . . breathing . . .

> *and then . . .*

> > *. . . I begin to weep.*

I curl into his shoulder as Ash holds and rocks me, his hand on my belly ever-present.

After a few moments . . .

"Get undressed," Ash says.

Through tears, I look up doubtfully.

"Come on, Stefanie, get undressed. I'm drawing you a bath."

Ash prepares a bath, extra hot, full of Epsom salts scented of lavender. He lights two candles and turns off the lights. As I soak, he brings me a cup of sleepy-time tea.

"No more caffeine, okay?"

I nod silently as Ash turns to leave.

"Stay . . ." I hear myself say and reach for his hand. *"Just for a little while, Sebastian . . . sit with me."*

Ash takes my hand, sits on the floor next to me, and kisses it.

His places his hand to the side of my face, and I incline my head into his palm. Caressing my cheek with his fingers, he lifts my chin and looks me in the eyes.

"You're going to be alright, Stefanie."

I recklessly suspend my disbelief.
My fabric's thread so frayed I barely breathe.
Unfailingly—neglect leads one to grief.
Perhaps it's only me whom I deceive?

—Seattle Airport, Dec. 21st, 12:38 p.m.

41
Montecito

I arrive at Marcus's mansion in Montecito by taxi straight from the airport. The entire flight over, my mind was defensively engaged, imagining one scenario after another.

Strategising and exploring side roads: I want no surprises, caveats, or contingencies left unaddressed. Best to make it short, sweet, and less painful—for the both of us.

Finally, during the taxi ride, it comes together. I go over and over it. I remind myself that I must assert control over the situation.

You are an adult woman, a professional. You have danced professionally since a teenager all over the United States and abroad.

I run through the choreography in my head and rehearse my lines like it's opening night.

He is expecting me, so he will be alone. I run down my mental checklist once again:

1. Tell taxi to wait.

2. Ring doorbell—just a formal business transaction.

3. Have ring in case, and case in hand.

4. Say: "Marcus, I want to thank you for your wonderful offer, but I can't in good conscious accept it."

5. Hand him the case.

6. Say: "I hope we can remain friends." (Remember to show sympathy!)

7. If he protests: "Marcus, I'm sorry, but I'm afraid I have made up my mind." (Be gentle but firm.)

8. Return to taxi and go home.

Done!

I can do this. I can actually do this. I'm no longer allowing others to define the situation. I begin to feel an inner reserve, a strength growing inside me. It is unfortunate—sad, even—but life goes on.

And a new life awaits me. I keep the image of that new life clear in my mind as I, case in hand, step out of the taxi.

"Thank you for waiting," I tell the driver. "I won't be a moment."

"Sorry, lady, I have another call," the driver says as I watch him pull away.

I tell myself it's nothing. I can always call an Uber from down the block.

I had assumed Marcus would be alone, but I look to find there are an unusual number of cars and vans out front and spilling down the street. People everywhere are bustling back and forth. The door is already open, and curious, I walk in.

Workmen are carrying items in through the front door out to the back patio. There is a table in the living room with catered food. Marcus is speaking with a woman who is taking notes and gesturing to the back.

He sees me. "Stefanie!"

He comes to give me a kiss, and I turn my head slightly at the last moment so it lands on my cheek.

"Sorry for the mess, I was hoping to have this completed by the time you arrived. I wanted to surprise you, but you know these things always take longer than expected."

I dread now that he has planned some sort of an elaborate welcome home party for me.

I'm already out of the book and I haven't even spoken.

"Marcus . . . what is all this?" I ask.

"Come with me, I want to show you," he says.

He takes me by the hand and leads me to the back patio. There I see that rows and rows of neatly aligned white chairs have been set up on a manicured lawn. They face a large trellis interwoven with vines and flowers that has been erected in front of a small stage.

My heart sinks.

"What do you think? It's really just a mock-up. But I wanted to see it to get a better idea, and of course, we need to choose what food will be served. What the band should play. I think I have a knack for this. I'm thinking of buying the company if they do a good job."

"Marcus!?"

"Stefanie, I wanted our wedding to be special."

"But . . . I said I needed a few days!"

"And you've had an entire week," he says reassuringly. "And anyway, I knew your answer the moment you took the ring with you."

42
Confrontation

As his implication registers, I'm suddenly disoriented. A canon goes off in my chest; I didn't know it could beat this hard. My mind races, and I start to panic. I tell myself this cannot be happening.

Suddenly cold, I wrap my arms around myself, and wonder if I'm going into shock. I feel my insides folding, liquefying, as if I'm turning inside out.

I've been forcibly ripped out of the pages of one story and pasted into another. A hostile one in which I don't belong or know the plot. My heart begins to fluctuate, and I lose the ability to speak.

Did I make a promise? Irrevocable, if not in word—in deed?

"Oh, and I have a little engagement gift. Look behind you."

With his hand, Marcus gestures to someone behind me. I hear it as it comes to life. Its growl is heavy and deep and angry. I turn to see its blood-red exterior is gleaming, confronting me with its presence.

I struggle and begin to hyperventilate. Unable to catch my

breath, I collapse into myself, into an emptiness created by the vacuum of where my "self" used to be and isn't anymore.

"She's a real beauty, isn't she? There's a lot of horsepower under that hood."

"Marcus," I whisper, trying to catch my breath.

"And you'll need to learn to drive a stick, of course."

"I need to say something."

"These babies don't come in automatics."

"Marcus . . . please stop."

As panic turns to frustration, adrenaline begins to course through my system. My body surges with each pulse, and my temples pound with each heartbeat.

"I've had Andre arrange some driving lessons for you."

"Marcus!?"

"Go slowly at first, and you'll be fine."

"Marcus, you're not listening to me." I'm contracted now, fists clenched, and my voice is beginning to quaver.

"Stefanie?" says Marcus, finally noticing my distress.

Then, to the housekeeper, "Roz! Call Dr. Anders, quickly, Stefanie is ill."

"Stop, Marcus—please."

"Stefanie, why don't you sit down."

Smouldering anger boils up, and I begin to seethe.

"Roz! Bring some water, quickly."

"Just listen to me—"

"Everything will be alright—" he goes on.

"Please, Marcus, let me—"

"Dr. Anders is on his way, and—"

I flash back to the *Tango* rehearsal: *Are you going to let a man tame you? This is your life, Stefanie—and it's time to fight. Right now!*

"Try to relax, Stefanie," he continues with calm assuredness. "After all, *I'm here to take care of you—"*

And at that . . . I unleash.

"Jezus Christus, Marcus! Just stop fucking talking!"

Workers and staff people turn towards us in surprise.

Heart racing and breathing sharply, I try to find my words and fail. Instead, I grab his wrist and place the case in his hand, closing his fingers around it.

"Marcus," I manage finally. Out of my eyes angry tears begin to flow. My voice quivers as I force myself on.

"Marcus . . . I am sorry, I *am*! But this is *not* going to happen—I cannot—I *will not* be another ornament to add to your collection. This wedding of ours, of yours . . . is not happening. It will *never happen!* I'm sorry, Marcus, I am very sorry . . . but there it is. Please accept this . . . *And let me be!*

Eyes wide and jaw open, Marcus appears to have turned into a mannequin version of himself.

I turn and trudge back through the house and out the front door. On the street, the taxi is idling, waiting for me.

"Other job was cancelled," the driver says. "I thought you may still need a ride."

43
The Proffer

In the taxi ride home, my nervous system is still in anarchy, firing frenetically in all directions, when Ambrose calls.

"Stefanie! Am I to assume you have returned?"

"Yes, Ambrose," I sigh.

Suddenly and without warning, I find myself exhausted beyond all reason. Physically depleted and emotionally arid, I have to fight sleep just to continue.

"Just back this morning," I manage.

"Excellent! Rumour has it that we may have lost Zoe to your old partner. Are we losing you as well?"

Ambrose's familiar jubilance helps to calm me.

Fresh from the debacle at Marcus's, I'm perhaps too forthcoming. But as nothing helps soothe my mechanism as giving it something else to work on, I open up.

"Honestly, Ambrose, I don't know about Zoe. She is still a couple months away from being in dancing shape, and she has other considerations now."

"Yes, I had heard, can't wait to meet the little one."

"At the moment, the ballet mistress position Sebastian offered works out well, assuming we have a season at all."

"Yes, I had heard about that as well—sad situation that. Listen, Stefanie, how about swinging by the villa? I have an idea I'd like to run by you. An idea that may benefit all of us."

* * *

From Ambrose's veranda, I call Sebastian.

He answers before I even hear it ring.

"Stefanie? Are you alright!?"

I hear the concern in his voice, but it will have to wait.

"Long story, Sebastian, and I don't want to get into the details at the moment, but yes, I'm fine. Listen, if you have a moment, I'd like you to speak with someone."

"Ahh . . . Okay, sure," Ash says a little tentatively.

I hand the phone to Ambrose.

"Hello, Sebastian, my name is Ambrose Thornhausen, and I would very much like to speak with you regarding a business opportunity . . . Yes, precisely. Would you be available for lunch, say tomorrow afternoon? . . . Yes, of course—I'd make all the arrangements to fly you down tomorrow morning. I'm sure Stefanie would love to see you . . . I'd rather go into details in person; however, let's just say it involves money for ballet. Let me put Stefanie back on the line."

"Ash?"

"Stefanie?"

"Ash, please come down. If nothing else, it's a free trip to Santa Barbara in the middle of a cold Seattle winter. I've spoken with Zoe, and Freddy already . . . Yes, I think it's important they be here too."

44
Santa Barbara

Sunday, December 22nd

"Baby food for Serafina, I presume?" asked Ash as he opened a kitchen cupboard to only to find it chock-a-block full of Zoe's brought-from-home Vegemite stash.

The following morning, we were in the kitchen of the flat Zoe and I shared on Anapamu. I was preparing food and indulging in some old-school point-shoe baking while Ash busied himself looking about the place.

"Do you actually eat this shi—eh, stuff?"

"Now and again," I smiled, looking up, "but I'll always be a Marmite girl at heart."

Ash twisted off the lid and took a tentative sniff. "Humph." He recoiled, grimacing. "Must be an acquired taste."

Due to the holiday season, Ambrose had chartered a morning flight, and the three of them arrived early. We'd planned to meet later and hear the proposal over lunch at the Fish Co.

Zoe and Freddy took the opportunity to get some coffee on

State Street, take a tour of the Mission, and possibly allow Ash and me some alone time.

"I didn't know you played chess," remarked Ash, browsing the titles on the bookshelf. He pulled out a well-worn paperback and began flipping through endless puzzles.

"Those are Zoe's—Freddy made the mistake of teaching her to play back at CCB."

"Mistake?"

I simply looked up from what I was doing and met Ash's eyes.

"Ahhh," he said and replaced the book. No further response from me was necessary.

"Speaking of Zoe," Ash mussed euphemistically as he looked in on Zoe's room, "I don't recall her being so—organised."

"With her permission, I gave her room the once-over while she was away."

"How long do you think it will stay that way?"

I just shook my head and laughed. "Entropy happens."

"Zoe happens!" added Ash.

If Ash thought my mind was an odd mixture of "insightful and lacking common sense," Zóza's mind was forever a mystery to me.

How could she store seemingly endless amounts of choreographic details in her mind, words in her head, and at the same time continually misplace her belongings, leave things behind, and when cloistered in a book, occasionally even forget to eat!?

And her room was a complete disaster! Or as Zoe herself liked to put it, a "serendipitous mayhem."

"I think of it as a continually evolving art installation," she justified to me one day. "I shall call it 'The Bedlam of Bell.'"

If Zóza and I had a single point of contention, this was it. Otherwise bringing a much-needed stability, harmony, and loving balance to my life, her proclivity for the dishevelled did tend to amplify the OCD in me.

As I prepared breakfast on the counter, I nonchalantly relate to Ash details of the previous day's melodrama. *Nonchalant* being the operative word. After all, I nearly have yesterdays fiasco boxed up and ready to place in the attic, *I just need to find an empty shelf.*

"So, as you can see," I say, keeping it light, "it didn't go exactly as planned."

Ash, concerned, parks himself down on a stool and looks at me.

"Stefanie, you had me so concerned yesterday—I know the whole situation was really distressing for you—having to face that—I'm so sorry. Tell me, how are you feeling now?"

"Are you trying to sort me out!?" I jest.

"Stefanie!" Ash nearly yells.

Knocked for six by the unexpected force in Ash's voice, I'm reduced to silence.

"You had me worried sick yesterday. I couldn't focus—on any-thing—the whole fucking day! I mean, really Stefanie—you were completely BSCB!"

"Perhaps I was a bit daft," I admit—grudgingly.

"BSCB" is an acronym Ash invented back in Capitol City to describe me—It stands for 'Bat Shit Crazy Ballerina.'

My inner bunhead cries out, *Why are the people I love are always yelling at me?*

Ash just looks at me and waits.

I resign myself to the fact he isn't going to let this go, so I take a breath and actually take stock of my feelings which, just below my facade, are still tender and longing to surface.

With tears welling up against my will, I ask, "Can I have cigarette at least?"

Ash stands and embraces me, then he takes my hand and leads me to the balcony. I collapse into a chair, pull my knees to my chest and with hands aflutter, fumble to light a cigarette.

"Well Stefanie?"

I take a long slow drag before continuing.

"I'm relieved—I am really. But still, I was this terrible—*this horrible ogre."* Brushing away tears I continue, "Though, as much as I would have preferred it to have gone differently, for me to exhibit a little class, a bit of posh, I am glad it's over."

"Is it?" Ash asks. "I mean, have you heard back or feel some sort of resolution?"

"There is still a bit there" I confess, "perhaps even more than a bit. I feel I need to make amends, as Freddy would say. But it will happen in its own time. Ash, *please*, I don't want to stress about it anymore right now. *Hey, are you hungry?*" I ask, more than ready to change the subject.

Without waiting for his response, I crush out the cigarette and I'm already sliding open the door when Ash, still seated, catches my arm, halting my progress.

He studies me for a moment. "I should have been here for you, Stefanie."

"You're here now." I glance back at him and smile. "Really, Ash, I'm okay—or at least I will be—okay?"

Stefanie, I think to myself, *you are nothing if not a master of compartmentalisation.*

"Okay, Stef," he sighs, acquiescing. "I suppose it's enough for now."

Back in the kitchen, I'm relieved to hear Ash himself change the subject—

"Hey, Stef, how about teaching me a little Dutch? I'm starting to feel like a monolingual American. Everyone speaks another language except me."

I smile to myself and decide now is not the time to tease him about his lack of French, despite his namesake. Instead I say—

"You know, I wasn't the greatest of teachers with Zoe."

"I'm not planning on becoming fluent today, just . . . can you tell me how to say hello?"

"*Hallo.*"

"I can remember that."

"Goodbye is '*Tot ziens.*'"

"Tater tot magazine."

"What?"

"I'm just trying to remember it."

"Okay, if it's easier, you can just say '*dag*' — rhymes with Bach." With mock condescension, I glance back over my shoulder. "You are familiar with the composer, aren't you?"

Ash just rolls his eyes, but my joust also lets him know that I really was better.

"You can use it for either. It means 'day,' but we use it casually for both hello and goodbye."

I was finishing up preparing breakfast on the counter and thus was fortunately already facing away from Ash when inspiration struck.

This would require some concentration and firm resolve. Wearing nothing like sensible shoes, I crossed my feet and brought one stiletto heel down on the top of the instep of my other foot and applied pressure just to the point of pain. Only then did I continue.

"A good toast," I went on, in as disinterested a voice as

possible, "for when you're out with friends, is '*neuken in de keuken.*'"

"Nuking in de cooking?" Ash attempts.

"More of a light 'N' than an 'ing.' Try saying it a little more casually, like Americans say 'drivin' or 'runnin' instead of driving and running."

"Nukin in de cookin?" he tries again.

"Better—but a bit more like 'no' and 'coke' and less 'new' and 'cook,'" I coached.

"Ahh so, like if we're out of cola?" Ash asked. "We have 'No Coke'? Okay, so, 'no-ken in de co-ken?'"

Close enough!

"Good," I say, and give myself an extra dig with my heel. "That works—*if you can remember it,*" I taunted.

"Well, as it turns out, we actually have 'no coke,' so yeah, I think I can remember. What does it mean?"

"Nightcap in the kitchen," I said casually as my mind spins a web of fabrications. "You know, a late-night drink before going to bed. But really, it's just something we say when toast. What does 'cheers' really mean, or '*skål*?'"

Seed planted, I lift my heel off my instep.

Turning towards him, seeing his hazel eyes in my flat leaves me suddenly feeling a little coquettish.

"Or, you could say . . . '*ik hou van je.*'"

"*Ik hou van je*?" Ash asks.

"*Ik hou van je*, Stefanie," I repeat quietly, looking into his eyes.

"*Ik hou van je*, Stefanie," he tries again.

"Here," I smile and take a chocolate from a bowl on the counter and hold it to his lips. "It means . . . 'may I have one.'"

"*Is that what it means?*" Ash says, accepting my offering. He's suspicious but continues to play along. "And so, if I want another one?"

"You have to say it again," I teased.

"*Ik hou van je.*"

"*Stefanie,*" I reminded.

"*Ik hou van je*, Stefanie," he said, smiling.

"That's really all the Dutch you need to know," I say, swaying back and forth like a schoolgirl and placing another chocolate in his mouth.

"That's always a nice thing to say."

Lowering his register while wrapping his arms around my waist, he repeated, "*Ik hou van je*, Stefanie."

As I incline my head and bring my arms around his neck to meet his kisses, "*Ik hou van je,* Sebastian," I whisper.

45
The Proposal

We spy Zoe and Freddy from outside the door of the Fish Co, holding hands and making eyes at each other as they slowly approached.

"Looks like they've been doing some 'catching up' of their own," Ash remarks.

"I think it's sweet," I say, my heart warming at the sight of them. "After knowing each other for such a long time, they finally—"

"Found each other?" Ash finished, pulling me close and kissing me.

"Well, hello, Miss Zóza," I say as they drew near. "Is *het wederzijds*?" (Is it mutual?)

"G'day, Stefanie."

She kisses me, then pulls away, and looks at me knowingly for just a moment with her soft brown eyes.

"Sir Frederik!" greets Ash in an over-the-top Scottish accent. "How was the Mission?" he says, holding the door open for them and smiling mischievously. "Tell me, my good man—were you able to 'ring the Bell?'"

Freddy shakes his head and chuckles slightly, shoots us a glance with pursed elvish lips, and lifts his brows as he, still holding Zoe's hand, follows her through the door.

"Vive la Santa Barbara!" he says quietly as he smiles and disappears inside.

Tables had been placed together, and Ambrose was seated at the head.

Mum greets Freddy and Zoe warmly. *"Wanneer ga ik die dochter van je eens ontmoeten?"* (When do I get to meet this daughter of yours?)

"Hi, Sophia. Soon—perhaps this afternoon?" replies Zoe, giving her a warm hug.

In addition to the four of us, Mum, Ambrose, and Nastya, there were three other people: two men and a woman. Potential board members or investors I assumed, as well as Connie accompanied by her new beau, Pablo.

Loquacious and scintillating, Nastya glided about the room making introductions. With effortless ease, she simultaneously beguiled, set at ease, impressed, and intrigued.

So that's her job?! I think to myself, finally beginning to understand this enigmatic young woman. Having become good friends with Nastya, and always knowing she was quite involved on the business side of things, I had never understood her precise role.

Clever, sophisticated, and the definition of grace, Nastya was a true debonair-ess.

"Freddy and Ash," said Ambrose, "allow me to introduce my wife, Anastasiia Mykolayivna Tereshchenko."

Ash politely introduced himself, but Freddy said, "Wow!— that's quite a mouthful."

"Nastya, please," said Nastya, "you should ask Ambrose his full name."

"Ambrose Dominic Damian Ignacio Conrad Thornhausen . . . the third," volunteered Ambrose with unselfconscious pride. "If you need a mnemonic device, the acronym spells *addict*."

Clearly amused, Freddy chuckles and shakes his head: appreciation of the elder prankster's humour showing through.

"And allow me," said Nastya to Ash and Freddy, "to introduce his lovely daughter, Constance. She and Pablo have just flown in from Spain."

"Hello, it's so nice to finally meet you," said Connie.

"Encantado," said Freddy, his natural charm bubbling forth, but just being Freddy.

Connie smiled and replied in Spanish, *"Entonces eres el famoso Frederik Danielsson, de quien tanto he oído hablar. No sabía que también hablabas español."* (So, you're the famous Frederik Danielsson that I've heard so much about. I didn't know you also spoke Spanish.)

"He's about to learn!" laughed Zoe, and Freddy actually blushed a little.

One reason I wanted Freddy and Zoe to join us in Santa Barbara was, if we were trying to lure them from established positions, Freddy with his full-benefit corporate job, and Zoe—well, honestly, I needed Zoe just for me—but having just flown her in from Australia, it hardly seemed right to abandon her in Seattle.

Not to mention Santa Barbara is our home, and without her presence our flat hasn't seemed a home in over a year. And if things did workout as I hoped, we would need to fly her down right away anyway.

I had quite the discussion with Ambrose following the "Marcus breakup catastrophe." I mentioned it would be wise to have experienced dancers he could trust in managerial positions.

Secondly was, given Ash's timidity with new people, especially when it was less than a casual situation, I wanted him to have the support of people he knew and trusted insofar as possible for the proposal. He's different, once he knows you. He can turn into quite the quipster once he feels comfortable.

Ash, always more comfortable in front of a crowd than in among them, was not the person to lead an outreach program, or drum up donations from potential benefactors and the like. He was naturally charming when he let you in. And, if necessary, he could summon it in emergency situations, but he found it exhausting, and difficult to keep up for long. In fact, the difference between him being outside the restaurant among only friends and inside the restaurant with strangers was noticeable.

Freddy, on the other hand, exuded confidence. And his charm, when he really turned it up, was nearly seductive. Something for the women patrons to dream about late at night as their husbands snored next to them on their beds or holed up till the early hours in their man caves.

And lastly, I had been sensing something was up between the Freddy and Zoe since our reunion lunch at Anthony's— and I felt that a mini-break weekend in Santa Barbara was just the gentle nudge required.

"I have followed your careers," Ambrose continued, "the four of you, for quite some time. It wasn't difficult as Zoe and Stefanie were right here under my wing. And I'm happy to see Frederik has rejoined the ranks of the living."

"Cheers!" said Freddy, holding up a diet coke.

"I suppose you could—" Ambrose went on. "Well, some would call me a balletomane. Been in love with dance for years. Started too late in life to really have much in the way of a career, but that never dulled my love of the art. Yes, it turned out my talent lies elsewhere, in finance.

"And I suppose that brings me to the reason I have summoned you all here. As you know I'm—*I was* the artistic director of the Montecito Ballet. And under my direction, we established ourselves as a world-class organisation.

"Not to put not too fine a point on it, but as of late it seems the board has rather ignominiously sacked me. They felt I exerted too much influence on the direction of the company.

What they fail to comprehend is that the majority of the company's funding and grants comes through my corporations. Companies inside companies. All legally loop-holed, of course. None of it comes back to me directly. Yet, I'm the one who ultimately pulls the trigger. It's all there in black and white, had they bothered to investigate in the first place. Of course, it's easier to accept money than turn it down, but occasionally *one should look a gift horse in the mouth.*

"This was never to be a permanent solution, of course. The idea was to encourage other companies to contribute by showcasing world-class performances and top-notch talent. I'm happy to add that under my direction, this objective had largely been achieved.

"Be that as it may, the withdrawal of my resources would essentially halve their yearly budget. Dancers would lose their jobs, take to hustling on the street, eating at soup kitchens, surviving in tent cities."

Nastya looks at me, shakes her head, smiles, and rolls her eyes. *"He is sooo enjoying himself,"* she whispers across the table.

"To get down to brass tacks," Ambrose continued, "the long and the short of it, Sebastian, is this. *I have a passion and an abundance of capital with no outlet—And you have a company with a distinct lack of funding."*

Ambrose let that sink in a moment before continuing.

"You would have to relocate to Santa Barbara. I didn't move from soggy old England to only live in the perpetual greyness of Seattle. That doesn't mean you couldn't have a Northwest presence, of course."

"What sort of influence would you exert over the company?" Ash inquired.

"Typical director control. That being said, Sebastian, it would relieve most of your headaches, teaching, fundraising. You would be free to focus on dance and choreography again.

"The details will all be spelled out in the contract. But you can see the type of dancing that interests me. Modern, classical, abstract—anything, really. As for my character, I'll let Zoe and Stefanie speak to that."

"No, Balanchine," said Ash.

"Ahh, yes," replied Ambrose. "Stefanie told me of your disfavour of Mr B. I can promise you the company will be Balanchine free. I think there are quite enough Balanchine companies to go around anyway."

Ash was silent, mulling it over. I was concerned. While I thought it was a good idea, Ash needed to arrive at that conclusion on his own—or not. And he had his pride, and so much invested into his own vision already.

"I want to be named assistant director," he said finally. "I want to choose my own staff, and I want guarantees that any dancer I have who chooses to relocate to Santa Barbara will have a salaried position in the company."

I was taken aback by Ash's forthrightness. Ambrose and Ash stared at each other, stone-faced, for what seemed an eternity. When the sides of Ambrose's face began to raise into a smile accompanied by a slight nod of his head.

"Let's drink to it!" Ambrose picked up a glass.

"Wait a moment!" said Mum. "We shouldn't toast a nameless company—it's bad luck."

"Santa Barbara Ballet, of course," I offered.

"I'm afraid, my dear," said Ambrose, taking my hand, "that name has already been taken. Any other suggestions? Anyone?"

"Zoe," Freddy asked, "what was the name of that huge tree you showed me this morning? It looked like something out of 'Lord of the Rings'—*Yes, Ash, we did do some sightseeing.*"

"The Moreton Bay Fig Tree!" said Zoe, "The Moreton Bay Ballet!?" she suggested.

"What about Moreton Bay Movement Theater, or Dance Theater?" suggested Freddy. "Make it less narrowly focused."

"My only concern is that folks won't know what a 'Movement Theater' is," Ambrose said. "Remember, this isn't New York City."

"Do not forget, we will be in competition with the Montecito Ballet, at least for a while," said Nastya. "Though I don't know if that is an argument for or against the 'Theater' epithet."

"Stefanie, Ash? Any thoughts?" asked Mum.

Ash thought for a moment, then said, "Honestly, I'm open to either, but linguistically, 'Bay' and 'Ballet' have a nice ring to it."

"Does anyone have objections to 'The Moreton Bay Ballet?'" asked Mum.

There was only silence from the table.

"Then it's settled!" Ambrose hefted his considerable weight from his chair. "Please raise a glass and join me in a toast to the newly minted Moreton Bay Ballet! *Cheers*, everyone!"

"*Nazdarovya*!" said Nastya.

"*Skål*!" said Freddy, lifting his coke.

"*Proost*!" said Mum.

Then Ash stood up . . .

I immediately realised that my clever joke was about to backfire and there was nothing I could do about it. A train wreck in slow motion. I close my eyes and remember being eleven . . .

"What a clever girl you are, Stefanie," Mum would say, her constant admonishment. "Perhaps you are . . . even a little too clever?"

Raising a glass to the ceiling, Ash exclaimed—

"Here's to '*Neuken in de Keuken*!" (Fucking in the Kitchen!)

Zoe burst out laughing, but Mum immediately turned to me and glowered.

Anticipating the fallout, I take cover by sinking down in my chair.

"Stefanie! Waarin geef je les Sebastian? Vanmorgen waren we bezig met wat keukenchoreografie, toch?" (Stefanie! What are you

teaching Sebastian!? Working on some kitchen choreography this morning, were we?)

Sensing something was up, Ash turned to me as well, his face reddening *What did you do?* he asked with his eyes.

I close my eyes and turn inside, preparing myself for the inevitable upwelling of emotions, only to find that I feel—nothing.

It's as if I've run out of embarrassment. The shame is absent. With all that has transpired in the last week, the last day, with Mum, with Marcus, this latest gaff is but a blip on the radar. No more than a mention on the back page. Mum's scolding seems to pass right through me.

I breathe deeply, and slowly, with determination, I rise from my chair and raise a glass of my own.

"Mum, quite honestly," I look around the table and settle on her last. Looking her right in the eyes, I continue, "It seems to me there would be a little less strife and misery in this world today, if, once in a while, we all were to stop grinding our axes and engaged in a little more *Neuken in de Keuken!!*"

The table was hushed, the restaurant fell silent, and for a moment the world rested on its axis in anticipation. Mum glared at me for a small lifetime, our eyes locked, and this time, I didn't turn away.

A glacial epoch later, Mum's glare began to melt. The sides of her face started to lift before she completely broke out laughing.

Nastya, amused at the goings-on asked, "What does it mean?"

Zoe, apparently having learned Ukrainian in her free time, leaned over to her and said quietly, *"Seks na kukhni,"* and Nastya began laughing out loud.

"Zoe!?" said Freddy. Zoe leaned and whispered in his ear, and he too began to laugh.

"Well, I don't know what it means," said Ambrose, "but anything that causes this much merriment sounds like a good name for my next Christmas ballet. Which reminds me, what is *our* first ballet to be?"

"Something dashing and romantic, I hope," added Mum, still laughing, showing a too-seldom-seen side.

"Agreed," said Ambrose. "In addition, it would contrast with the Montecito Ballet's increasingly turgid repertoire." Then, turning to me, he whispered, "I hear they're planning an entire season of Balanchine," and winked.

"When are we planning to open?" asked Zoe.

"I think we should plan for late spring or early summer at the latest," replied Mum. "We'll need some time to find facilities, establish ourselves, and convene a new board."

"It's nothing that can't be greased with small injection of capital," added Ambrose.

"We're going to need brochures, photos, a website," said Freddy. "If you don't have someone in mind, I'd like to toss my friend Nick Johnson's name in the hat."

"Nick's good," Ash nodded in agreement. "I can show you the website he did for us."

"I've seen it. Papa, you should have a look," said Connie.

"Everything is possible," added Nastya. "And on that note, would you excuse us a moment?"

Watching the ladies make their way en masse to the powder room, as I leave the table, I overhear Ambrose remark—

"What a plenitudinous plethora of pulchritude."

"Isn't that redundant?" asked one of the new board members, perhaps feeling the need to impress.

Without ever redirecting his gaze, I hear a well-pleased Ambrose growl, *"Who the bloody cares?"*

After paying the bill, additional chit-chat, tossing out of suggestions, and general camaraderie, Ash, who had been thinking to himself for some time, stood and announced—

"I think I have an idea."

46
Moreton Bay

After lunch, Ash wanted to see our company's "name tree," so upon leaving the restaurant we leisurely walk the short distance hand in hand. As we neared the tree, while it was still out of sight, I asked Sebastian to close his eyes and I guided him the rest of the way.

Zóza and I had loved this tree ever since Nastya first showed it to us. Every couple of weeks, we would make a point of visiting, grabbing a sandwich along the way to picnic beneath its boughs.

We had always felt they should build a park around it, and discussed it often. As it was, however, it stood on the corner of Chapala and Montecito near both the bus and train stations with Highway 101 just over a barrier.

With the tree as its centrepiece, we reimagined a new lusher landscape to frame it. Perhaps a playground and some picnic tables in the distance, more trees, and flowers and vines. Remove the streets, and most of all, do something with that awful freeway. I was not at all surprised Zóza included this on her sight-seeing excursion with Freddy.

"Open your eyes."

"Holy Jesus!" Ash exclaimed, opening his eyes and revelling in its immensity.

I watched Ash as he circled carefully around the tree. The visible root structure alone spread nearly as far as its branches. The majesty of its leaves ever-shading him as he ambulated around its circumference.

"What do you think?" I asked, knowing what Ash thought but wanting to hear it anyway.

"I think we need a silhouette of this as our company's symbol. Make some T-shirts at least," Ash said enthusiastically.

"Thank you, Stefanie," he said completing his circle, putting his arm around me and kissing me on the temple. "Stefanie, I don't really have the words—can't do it justice. You know, in Chico, we had a famous tree called the Hooker Oak, and there was a park around it. They used it in the film *Robin Hood*, with Errol Flynn back in the thirties. 'The Gallows Oak' is what they call it in the film. It since has fallen—nothing but a trunk remains. I wish I could have shown it to you.

"Stefanie, this has been such a crazy, amazing . . . what has it been? Just a week? I feel like it's moving so fast, I want to slow down and breathe in each moment."

"Oh!" he said, pulling away slightly and giving me a mercurial look. "That reminds me." I felt his mood shift from awe to sarcasm. "Speaking of moments. *Nice one at lunch, by the way.*"

"Sebastian . . ." I whimpered, "I'm so sorry. In my mind I thought . . . I was thinking you might use it as a toast tonight when the four went to dinner. I was only thinking of making Zoe laugh. When you stood up at lunch, I swear to god I almost died."

"Oh, Zoe laughed alright!"

"Ash . . ." I pleaded mercy.

He laughed, smiled, and slowly shook his head as he embraced me. "Still, you were quite impressive. Have you ever spoken to your mother that way?"

"Never! But honestly, I had nothing to lose. Emotionally, all my angst had been spent."

"Good for you, Stef. Nevertheless, watch your back woman!" he joked. "The score is tied, 'one all' —*for now."*

47
Tied!?

I'm taken aback by his assertion. Did Ash think he won our little joust at the studio? I wondered now about the wisdom of my reluctance to nail the coffin shut during the other day's rehearsal.

Humph—tied indeed.

My competitive streak now engaged, I pushed him away and challenged him with a squint.

"Bring it on, cowboy!"

Ash laughs haltingly, surprised by my sudden change of mood.

"Anytime, girlfriend," he counters. "Anytime, anywhere!"

"As if!"

"Okay, *okay*!—Stop, timeout, enough," said Ash, making a "T" sign with his hands and trying to put a stop to it before we really got going. But he was laughing so hard he had to put his hands on his knees.

"Stef, please—I can't take it. Let us live to joust another day. Deal?"

"Pussy!" I taunted.

At my so uncharacteristic turn of phrase, Ash fell to the lawn rolling in stitches, and I, now laughing as well, happily fell on top of him.

48
Genesis

"So, what's this idea of yours?" I ask.

We sat on the ground, legs stretched and crossed. After a few minutes, Ash's head finds its way to my lap, and I gently stroke his hair as he gazes up and marvels at the sun drops sparkling through the wind caressed leaves.

"Interesting that you should ask," he smiled.

"Robin Hood? Zorro?"

"Something along those lines—with some swordplay, but I'd prefer to do something original."

"Isn't Freddy good at fencing?"

"Well, he is amazing at stage play."

"And Zoe?"

"I don't know, but this is Zoe we're talking about."

"True," I said.

"Still," said Ash, "I worry about the languidly of her movement."

"Look," I say, "Zoe gets type cast in rolls by choreographers who see her dance in one piece and want the same quality of movement in their own work."

"So?"

"So, they use her and get what they were looking for. Then another choreographer sees her in that piece and the process starts all over again. That doesn't mean that's all she can do—you never saw us perform *Duet*, and don't forget that night she mimed the Tyson fight. What are you thinking, Ash?"

"Us."

"What do you mean?"

"The way we verbally spar with each other, but told through the vehicle of sword play."

"I'm listening," I say.

"Say it's a famous sword master's school and Zoe plays his daughter. She isn't supposed to learn to fence, but out of love for his daughter, he teaches her the art of the blade. Maybe there is a competition to compete for her hand in marriage—"

"But she takes part as well?"

"Exactly, or something like that—she defeats the best!"

"Or," I say, getting excited, "if they are romantically involved—she lets him win."

Might as well keep it true to life, I muse, but don't say out loud.

"Ohh, you're good!"

"But Ash . . ."

There was something that didn't feel right to me—it wasn't a big thing, nothing insurmountable.

"The sword master may be revered," I continued, "yet I can't see men competing for the hand of a sword master's daughter, not like they would for royalty. Not like they would for the hand of a princess."

Ash squishes up his face. "Point taken, Miss 'Rain on My Parade' Janssen—but point taken."

"What about this," I interject. "The sword master was many years ago the queen's personal guard, entrusted to protect, at all costs, her most valuable possession, her daughter the princess."

"Go on." Ash has sat up now, our creativity spurring each other on.

"Over time, the princess and the sword master fall in love, but alas, it cannot be, as she is betrothed to another."

"Ohh," said Ash, "I like where this is headed, please continue."

"He becomes her—she's now the queen—secret lover and the father of her child, which makes his child—a princess!"

"So, the queen," Ash continues, "allows her from a young age to spend time with, unbeknownst to her, her real father and thus he trains her in secret. What about the king?"

"He's an idiot," I say. "We'll kill him off or something, maybe make him a buffoon, comic relief."

"Okay, okay, I like it, but there is also a possibility here, that he finds out of his queen's betrayal—"

"And?"

"I don't know, but—someone's going to have to die."

"This is starting to get deep," I say. "Do you think it's too heavy for a summer children's ballet?"

Ash reflected for a moment, then shrugged. *"Fuck 'em—this is art!"*

I laugh out loud.

"Alright, alright," Ash relents. "Let's say this tragedy takes place in the distant past. Maybe the sword master kills the king, or he dies in a tragic accident."

"Flash forward," I say, inspired, "and now we have our young princess. Playful, light, and carefree, she craves adventure rather than being a confined proper girl."

Ash: "So she puts on a mask so as not to be recognised and seeks to right wrongs, fight injustice. Loved by her real father, but again put into a betrothal bind—"

Stef: "Which is problematic for her, as on one of her adventures she meets a like-minded young gentleman—"

Ash: "Also with mask!"

Stef: "Of course! Eventually she discovers his true identity and allows him to win their final showdown, and at the same time, her hand in marriage! And what else?"

Ash: "And—and hijinks ensue! We can hammer out the details later."

"Will you do the choreography?" I asked.

"That's not the question," said Ash. "The question is, who will do the fight choreography?"

"What about Freddy? You said he's good," I ask.

"He is, and he would do a competent job, but he's our lead, and will be assisting with so much else with the new company; I think it would be too much of a burden. Also, I'm thinking as this is our opening ballet. Maybe we need to bring in a ringer."

"Who did you have in mind?"

"We need Bruce King."

Sebastian met Bruce King during Thomas Hargrove's production of *Carmen*. Bruce was a teacher of ballet, chore-ographer, fight master, and connoisseur of all things art.

49
Disclosure

It's evening now, and the day's pageantry has quieted. Hand in hand, Sebastian promenades me slowly along the pier. The sun's setting rays cast auburn hues against an ambiance of august clouds, overlaying a firmament watercolour of cerulean. I feel at peace.

"Sebastian . . ." I pondered, "What if I *hadn't* wandered into the bookshop that afternoon?"

Ash leads me over to the edge of the pier and, leaning on the railing, gazes out to the Pacific, his hair tossing slightly in the breeze.

Quietly, he says, "I would have found you, Stefanie."

I join him on the railing and sarcastically ask, "And how exactly would you have managed that?"

Taking my hand on the railing, Ash turns towards me. His forehead crinkles, and his concerned hazel eyes silently take me in. The excitement of our earlier inspiration has passed. Ash is quieter, but he also seems somewhat hesitant— perhaps even slightly withdrawn.

"What I mean, Stefanie, is, well—let's just say it wasn't entirely by chance . . ." Ash trails off.

With his hesitancy, the moment has become emotionally weighted. Intrigued by his reluctance, and suddenly a little apprehensive myself, I prompted him—

"Come on, Ash, out with it—*use your words.*" I repeat Ash's words to me at brunch in an attempt to lighten the mood, but my apprehension remains.

"Stefanie . . ." He sighed hesitantly, *"I knew you were coming."*

"How could you?" I asked, perplexed and at the same time somewhat relieved. "I didn't even know I was coming until practically the day before."

Taking a breath, Ash continued, "When your mother emailed the Weston to confirm an adjustment in her reservation, a double room now, as you would be accompanying her—"

"Yes!?" I asked, unsure where this was going.

"She cc'd my company's email—"

"She what!?" He had my attention now.

"I almost deleted it, thinking it was travel spam or an email gone astray, but in the subject line, I read the name—Janssen."

My head begins to spin—the gears begin their churn.

"Listen," he continues, "that was it. No personal notes or phone calls. Not even a hello. Just the bare facts of your itinerary and where you would be staying. I think it was your

mother's way of telling me, 'Look, here is a piece of information—what you do with it is up to you.'"

"I've always liked your mom," Ash went on, shaking his head,
and with a tentative smile he added, "You know, Stefanie, in
her own way, she's as scheming as you are."

Mum!? My mechanism comes full stop.

My mind completely emptied, I stand and face the Pacific.
Entirely taken aback, for a moment I'm nothing but the cool
ocean breeze, the sound of the waves crashing upon the
shore, and the beckoning call of seagulls flying overhead.

Then—slowly, the synapses start to fire, the connections
begin to reveal patterns. The subtext between the lines
that I, too caught up with my own story, hadn't bothered to
notice: subtle indications which, with the benefit of hindsight,
become unequivocally clear.

Mum's insistence on my accompanying her on her trip. "A
little space to think over the engagement," she had said—as
if leaving Santa Barbara to travel to Seattle in the middle of
winter was anyone's idea of a holiday.

Ash's non-reluctance at our brunching with Mum, despite
my obvious distress . . . and otherwise so entirely out of
character for him.

Even Mum's comment about Ash's availability, which in my
state of mind at the time, sailed right past me.

And in the hotel room—in spite of her scolding—giving
me her approval of both Ash and an extra week to spend
with him.

And lastly, how exactly did Ambrose know anything about the difficulties facing Ash's company if he hadn't spoken with Mum?

Frankly, I didn't know what to think. Should I be angry? She had been pretty hard on me, after all—and she had set it up!

And yet, would I have had the temerity for once, to face my past and start anew without her? Hmmm.

Am I grateful? . . .Yes.

Slowly, it begins to dawn on me. My elbows on the railing, I place my face in my hands. It occurs to me that without Mum, none of this would have been possible.

There would be no new company, no reunion with dear friends. No burgeoning romance between Freddy and Zoe . . . No Sebastian.

I look out over the Pacific and breathe in the cool salty ocean breeze as it caresses my face. Then I close my eyes and feel nothing but awe at her guiding hand in all this.

My eyes well up as the warm rush of a mother's love for her only daughter—at times so seemingly distant, but now so blindingly apparent—sweeps over me in waves.

A love perhaps at times so difficultly—so inexplicably— expressed, but nevertheless, so very achingly present.

"She knows me better than I know myself," I say quietly, under my breath.

"Stefanie?" Ash asked, unable to hear my mumblings, and concerned about my reaction.

I wipe my tears with my hand and return to the present, only to find my poor dear Ash tensely waiting with concern.

I reach up and touch his cheek with the palm of my hand and brush some hair back over his ear. Then I take a moment to adjust his collar and straighten his tie.

At first, I intend to console him as he has so often consoled me this past week. I want to reassure him that I don't in any way feel betrayed and that when it comes to keeping little secrets to himself, *he really must learn to step up his game.*

Then it occurs to me, there's a better way to alleviate his anxiety.

"So, Sebastian . . ." I say, shaking off the tears and smiling mischievously, "You were stalking me."

"Huh!?"

"Sebastian, you just admitted you were stalking me, there's no two ways about it. Sebastian 'the Stalker' Soulier."

"Honestly, Stefanie," he smiled in relief, "I was just trying to get up the nerve to go knock on your door when you wandered in the bookstore."

* * *

As we continued our walk along the pier, a nagging remainder kept nudging me, a small piece of unresolved that I'm unable to let go.

"Sebastian . . ."

It's too soon for this, and I don't want to distress him further, but we're "right here," and after seven years, I simply have to know.

"You never answered my question," I continued.

Ash shakes his head. "What question is that?"

"Why did you leave? Why did you leave me, Sebastian?"

Ash sighed a long exhalation. "I think . . ."

Ash paused and considered long before beginning again.

"I think, I convinced myself that if it was going to happen with us, it would have happened by then. We had this game of romantic musical chairs, you and I . . . and I got tired of always being caught standing up.

"And Stefanie, don't forget you *were* seeing someone. I was never quite sure what to do with that. It's as if one of us was always involved at the wrong time. If one of us was available, the other was in a relationship.

"Perhaps you were madly in love, I didn't know. It hardly seemed like a loving thing to do to insert myself into some weird situation and put you under a lot of emotional stress with my own wishes . . . which, I suppose, is exactly what I did this last weekend.

"But Stefanie that's why—"

"What happened to 'all's fair in love and war?'" I challenged.

Ash didn't respond immediately. But looking me in the eyes and taking a moment to brush some hair behind my ear, he went on.

"As for love and war, I try not to base my choices in life on idioms, though I don't know. Perhaps in this case . . ." Ash hesitated. "But placing you in the middle and causing such emotional turmoil, especially knowing your dislike of confrontation hardly seemed to me like a loving thing to do. That's why—this time, Stefanie—I simply didn't want to know.

"Anyway, when the PSB offer presented itself, well . . . James had money and a future he could offer. You know, actual solidity. What did I have to offer? A dancer's wages, no savings. If I landed wrong on a jump, it could be the end of my career. I just thought you deserved more than that.

"I started having second thoughts from the beginning of the *Tango* rehearsals, and by the night at the party—well, by that time my plans had been set, flight booked, contract accepted.

"I—that is, Stef, had I known that those last few weeks . . ." He takes a moment then sighs, "Stefanie . . . I don't know what I'm trying to say."

I turn to face him and kiss his lips.

"Sebastian . . . you just said it!"

50
Revelations

Later that evening, Zoe and I drove her Beetle over to Mum's house to introduce her to Serafina. My appreciation—awe, actually—of Mum's influence had been slowly sinking in all afternoon.

Opening the door, Mum, warm and welcoming, invited us in.

"Oh! Look at her, she's the spitting image of her mother!" Mum exclaimed. "What is she, about four months now?"

"She will be, in another week or so," answered Zoe.

Mum picked Serafina up and held her close. She sang to her quietly and rocked her gently in her arms. I look at Mum now with fascination; having no younger siblings, this was an image I hadn't seen before. Walking about the room, an infant in her arms, cooing and making faces. Did she do that with me? Of course she must have, and long before she became the self-made woman she is today.

When Mum arrived in England, she didn't have much more than the clothes on her back, the shoes on her feet—and me, an infant no older than Serafina to take care of.

At least that was the story I'd always been told—and when Mum felt I was being unappreciative, endlessly so. And by the time I was a teenager, no longer exactly poor, I gave the story the short shrift of an adolescent.

Now watching Mum with her soon-to-be great-goddaughter, my heart broke open for her and her own life struggles. Imagine, alone in a foreign country, certainly hungry. A baby to feed, little money, and fewer prospects.

I close my eyes and sigh as the realisation silently dawns . . . *God, I've been such a self-centred twaat.*

When Zoe goes to put Little Stef down for a nap, I realise I need to take this opportunity to speak with Mum—my heart opening to her as in hadn't in such a long while.

"Mum," I say, and she turns to me.

"Mum I . . ." With emotions bubbling up, I have trouble finding my words.

"Yes, Stefanie?"

"Mamma . . ." I switch to Dutch, and my name for her when I was little.

She lifts her brows, amused.

She's been "Mum" since I was ten. It's been nearly twenty years since I've called her "Mamma."

I don't switch so Zoe won't overhear; Zoe knows everything, anyway. Even if she didn't understand Dutch, Zóza can feel emotions through a wall and can read people's moods like a book—and of those she loves the most, especially so.

I use Dutch because it's "our" language, and my only language for the first years of my life, and for a while I thought, until she first travelled with me as a little girl back to Utrecht, our own private language.

"*Wat is het*, Stefanie?" (What is it, Stefanie?)

Mum has been a mountain in my life; always there, at times insurmountable, but now alive with warmth. Beginning to sob, I walk towards her and embrace her, feeling her strength, her aliveness.

"*Mamma—Ash heeft het me verteld.*" (Mamma—Ash told me.)

She embraces me warmly for a moment, then holds my face in her hands. She looks at me and brushes my tears away with her thumbs. Sensing my vulnerability, she doesn't even bother to deny it.

In Dutch she says, "I just gave it a nudge, Stefanie—that's all, just a nudge. Don't you see? You are my life, Stefanie. My only daughter. How could I stand by and do nothing when I saw how joyless you had become?"

As we continue to embrace, Zóza carrying Serafina in her arms emerges from the bedroom; both she and Little Stef are silently weeping. And we gather the both of them in our embrace.

Then hearts and hands begin to intertwine.
Awakening—thy touch, I find thee near.
How hath thou tamed the chaos of my mind?
Wherefore thy presence so subdues my fear?

—Awaiting dawn, Jan 10th, 5:36 a.m.

51
Amends

"*Sokil sokil, Ya hnizdo!*" (Falcon falcon, this is nest!)

I hear Zóza's voice through my mobile. Despite what lay before me, I couldn't help but laugh at her antics.

"*Sokil sokil, Ya hnizdo*" was our "secret code"—it was some line from a Soviet-era spy film we had watched recently with Nastya—and Zoe was having endless amounts of fun with it.

"Stevie—has the rabbit reached his warren?"

I stood just around the corner from the cafe where, mobile in hand, I had arranged to meet Marcus. Making amends with Marcus was something that had been pressing on me for a few weeks now. I wasn't so reluctant to do it, just unsure of how to approach it without making things worse.

"Seven minutes, Zóza," I say into the phone. "Just give me seven minutes—no more and no less."

"I read you loud and clear, Stevie—Marcy magpie's fledgling flight will launch from nest in T-minus seven minutes—over and out."

235

Did I mention how much I love Zóza?

Marcus was sitting in the cafe and stood somewhat formally as I approached. We embraced, a little stiffly, and sat down.

Despite everything, upon seeing him again, now somewhat diminished, I felt a certain amount of guilt. After all, Marcus wasn't a bad person; there are no villains in this story. He was just being Marcus. Young, entitled, and successful, bending the world to suit his whims. And why should getting married be any different? I wondered if my refusal was the first time in his life things hadn't gone his way.

"I ordered you a vanilla latte," Marcus says, holding up a cup. "It's still your favourite, right?"

I tried for a smile; in truth, I had never liked flavoured coffee.

"I'm surprised you called, actually," he continued. "I hear you're involved with the new company. Have a new . . . relationship."

"Marcus . . ." I began.

Other than the upcoming "cafe choreography," this time I was improvising. I had only a vague notion of what I would say. I was "being present in the moment," as Ash would say. Taking it as it came.

I take a deep breath and just let it out. "Marcus, I wanted to apologise to you—in person. Really, I am *so very sorry* for what happened. My behaviour that day was unforgivably rude . . . and I'm sorry."

Marcus looked down for a moment before glancing up at me. "Are you happy, Stefanie?"

I look at him and nod. "I am, Marcus . . . I am happy."

"Good," he says, nodding his head, looking at nothing in particular. "Sooo, tell me about this new chap of yours."

It was a probing question, but the worst part was over; now was the time to make things better. *But tread lightly, Stefanie.*

"Well, his name's Sebastian, and he's not exactly 'new.' I've actually known him for . . ." I think back. *What has it been? Eight or nine years?*

"Almost a decade," I say slowly.

"Was he the reason?" he asks, not quite ready to let it go.

I sigh, turn towards him, and allow myself to take his hand. Against every impulse in my body, I remind myself, *Just be honest, Stefanie, he deserves that much, at least.*

"No, Marcus. *In truth, he was a catalyst,* but honestly, I was losing myself."

"I just wanted to give you a dream life, Stefanie. I thought you wanted it too."

"I thought I did, Marcus—for a time, but it turns out, I'm just not built that way."

Just say it, Stefanie

"Marcus, I know you only meant well, and at first, I'll admit I was taken in by all the pomp and circumstance. The glamour of it all. But after a while, I felt like I was drowning—like I was being smothered in all your care. Quite honestly, I wouldn't know what to do with myself with an such idle life. I need challenges, obstacles to overcome, or else I become sullen and despondent."

"Listen, Marcus," I continue, "the fact of the matter is, I'm an unapologetically moody, impulsive, capricious artist—*and I have absolutely no intention of ever changing.* I need someone who understands that about me—but perhaps most of all . . ." I pause and look at him. "*I'm in love. Will you forgive me?*"

After a moment's pause, he deigns, "Of course, Stefanie, I forgive you."

And as if on cue—which actually it was—Zoe entered the cafe "stage left" to pick up some lattes and snacks for the company. And assisting Zoe, trailing along just behind her, followed Marcy.

52
Scheming Emmas

Early after Moreton Bay Ballet officially opened its doors, though still in our temporary location, a talented young dancer joined the ranks of the company.

She was quite a pretty, twenty-ish, flirty little thing who went by the name of Marcy Van der Kamp.

I think she spelled her name with a "y"—though I wouldn't be at all surprised to learn she spelled it with an "i" and dotted it by drawing a little heart over the top.

And despite her surname, she spoke zero Dutch: something I ascertained rather quickly by her blank stare upon our introduction.

She was incessantly soliciting "advice" from the men in the company, but more specifically, she directed her attentions towards both Freddy and Ash.

While I'm happy to report neither of them encouraged her in any way, Sebastian had a more difficult time of it, as he was always trying to be polite and helpful, but was frankly uncomfortable, not used to being put in such a position.

Freddy, on the other hand, a seasoned and consummate charmer, found the entire situation endlessly amusing.

One day during rehearsals, while observing "Man-eater Marcy" (as Zoe and I guiltily referred to her) make her rounds, Zoe said to me, "Stevie—please tell me that wasn't me ten years ago."

I laughed a little and shook my head. "You were never that needy—though, I think at some point, we're all a little like that, but no Zóza—that was never you."

It occurred to me now that Zoe and I were the veteran dancers. We were the ones everyone looked up to. As I was considering retiring only a few weeks previously, the insight should have been unremarkable, yet I had not thought of it in quite this way before.

Recalling my own anxieties at that age, I continued, "She's probably just insecure, so she seeks validation of her self-worth from others—especially men. Marcy needs the reassurance."

"Marcy needs to get laid," said Zoe.

I burst out laughing—loud enough that several dancers rehearsing glance in our direction.

After a few further moments of observing her, Zoe says, "You know Stevie, I think she just wants someone to take care of her."

And with that, I glance up and turn toward Zoe, only to find her turning to face me—a light bulb going on for both of us.

"Marcus!" we say simultaneously.

* * *

As choreographed, Zoe spies us from the counter. She walks over to our table to say hello while waiting for her order—Marcy in tow.

"Zóza! I thought you were rehearsing," I recite my line.

"G'day, Marcus," says Zoe.

"Hey, Zoe." Marcus stands and they have a perfunctory embrace. "It's been a while. How was Australia? Did you just get back?"

"Just before Christmas, actually. My parents were a little nonplussed at the timing, but," Zoe looked at me as she put her hand on my shoulder, "Stevie needed me—so here I am."

Then, turning more toward me, she continued . . .

"Freddy and Bruce need some time to work out a few things in the village scene, so Ambrose sent us out to get: One, lattes for the company, and two—" Zoe lifted her arms as if conducting, and together, to the tune of "For He's a Jolly Good Fellow" we chanted rhythmically—

"A steamed milk and honey for Bruce!" ending with a clap of our hands.

We said it as if we had done it many times, as if it was "a thing" between us. In fact, we had just made it up earlier that morning—and as neither Marcus nor Marcy had seen it, they were both surprised and amused, which is precisely the impact we were hoping for.

A little carefree gayety to set the mood.

Up to this point Marcy was, as intended, standing a little behind Zoe and a little to her left, somewhat uncertain, and thus far ignored.

"Marcy!" I exclaimed, turning my attention to her all at once, "I don't believe the two of you have met. Allow me introduce you to Marcus."

"Marcus and I are—old friends." I say, giving Marcus's hand a final squeeze before letting it go. "He's a great patron of the arts, has exquisite taste—"

"And he's fabulously wealthy," whispered Zoe.

"Hello," said an enchanted Marcy.

"Don't listen to them," said Marcus, becoming his old self again, "though every word of it is true," he winked.

"Marcy here is our company's new 'rising star'—isn't that right, Stevie?" said Zoe.

"We're grooming her," I added demurely.

Now receiving exactly the kind of validation which she had for several weeks sought, Marcy actually started glowing.

"Unfortunately," Zoe continued, her soft brown eyes turning to me now, "Marcus has recently had his heart broken by a brilliant, beautiful, but complicated woman of artistic inclination and is currently leading an affection-less existence."

"That . . . is also true," said Marcus, though casting a suspicious glance in my direction.

Marcus was many things, but stupid was not among them.

"Oh, I'm so sorry to hear that," said Marcy genuinely.

Their order completed, Zoe and Marcy went to the counter.

Marcus turned towards me and looked at me knowingly for a moment.

"Well, Stefanie, she's very pretty—and young! Exactly what are you up to, Stef?"

"I haven't the faintest idea what you're talking about," I say, feigning exasperation.

My accent tends to become sharper and more pronounced when I'm not being entirely truthful. The slight hint of estuary vanishes completely. It's an obvious poker tell—but then again, I don't play poker.

"Honestly, Marcus, sometimes your flights of fancy are really more than one should have to endure." Then, glancing in his direction, I whispered, "But speaking of fancy—*do you?*"

Marcus squinted at me as Zoe and Marcy returned briefly to say goodbye. Marcus rose from his chair, enveloped Marcy's hand in both of his, and looked her directly in the eyes.

"It was most enchanting to meet you, Marcy," said Marcus, his innate suave on full display. "When will I be able to see you perform?" he continued, not letting go of her hand.

Following a prolonged silence on Marcy's part, Zoe answered for her.

"You can drop by the studios anytime."

Marcy 'Deer in the Headlights' Van der Kamp had apparently lost the power of oratory.

"Tell me," said Marcus, "is that Marcy with a 'y' or with an 'i?'"

"With an 'i,'" Marci managed, her eyes positively beaming.

"Well, Marci with an 'i' . . ." Marcus went on, deepening and softening his voice, *"may you continue to dance on in my imagination, until by such grace, shall my eyes receive the pleasure."*

Having lost all verbal facility, and with her hand still enveloped within Marcus's, Marci nonetheless impresses me by performing a slow, elegant curtsy.

"Coffee is cooling," says Zoe. "Come on, Marci—let's move."

Zoe kisses me on the cheek and heads out the door with Marci floating along behind her.

"Laying it on a little thick, aren't you?" I say.

"You're one to talk . . . but, nicely done, Stefanie."

Marcus watched Marci exit the cafe and turn down the street. When she glanced back over her shoulder only to find Marcus still observing her, she actually skipped.

"Nicely done indeed," he repeated, smiling.

53
Couture

February 6th was my thirtieth birthday, and I was feeling somewhat forlorn about it, when Zoe gave me a birthday gift that I will never forget.

Shortly after we introduced Marci to Marcus, she was seen driving a new car and sporting rather expensive outfits outside of rehearsal.

With the spring of romance and her newfound prosperity apparently serving as some sort of life validation, Marci went rather quickly from the tiresome habit of pursuing approval to the even more tiresome habit of feigning benevolence and giving advice rather than soliciting it. Well—more of a repertoire add than a change, really.

If there was nothing to constructively critique, she would offer "encouraging" motivational shout-outs: "Well done, Zóza! It's really coming along Stevie!" (Yes, she calls us by our affectionate names for each other—we shall refrain from going there.)

While no doubt well intended, and serving as a means to ingratiate herself to us, as both Zoe and I were en pointe by the time she was born and had been dancing at least semi-professionally to some degree by the time she took her first dance class (actually, by that time, I'd probably even won the) . . . well, you get the idea.

Anyway—this was good-naturedly tolerated, but only to a point. And one day, following a few weeks of this sort of behaviour, my dear sweet Zóza had had just about all she could stand.

Marci, though finished rehearsing for the day, came back to the studio to "display" and garner some additional attention. She parked her new convertible in the disabled spot—which incidentally happened to be the best place to view it from inside the studio.

"Stevie, what in god's name have we done?" Zoe asked.

"Countess Kamp-ula exists, Zóza—and we have ourselves to thank for it," I reflected, laughing just a little.

"A validation vampire," Zoe nodded in agreement, "able to suck all breathable air out of the room in a single flirt."

"Now, apparently, she's also a wench of wisdom," I laughed.

"Nurturing nympho," Zoe smirked.

"Helpful harlot?" I offered.

"Counselling coquette!" added Zoe.

"Compliment courtesan!" I laughed.

"We have to stop it, Stevie," cautioned Zoe.
"Marci's coming—again."

I inclined my head over to Zoe and whispered in her ear, *"Not with Marcus she's not!"*

"Ohh!" Zoe's cried, her face lighting up as she turned to me. Then she hugged me and laughed on my shoulder.

Marci entered through the glass doors, spotted us, and struck a pose,

"Hi, girls! What are we up to today?" she asked, all smiles.

Suddenly, I got the impression that perhaps Marci thought Zoe, Nastya, Connie, and I constituted some sort of club—to which she had recently been extended a gold membership. *Jeetje!* (Oh dear!)

"Marc Marc and I are throwing a Valentine's Day bash down at the Ponderosa, and we want everyone to come!" chimed Marci.

Marc Marc!? Ponderosa!?

"Dates and times are all on the flyer," she said as she handed us two. "Oh, and the big news is—Marcus is joining MBB's Board of Directors!—Isn't that amazing?"

"Why—that is big news," I said, genuinely surprised—and doing my best to appear pleasantly so.

"Can I ask you two a question?" Marci pleaded. "You both have such sophisticated taste, I wanted to ask . . . Marcus just bought it for me, what do you think?"

"The car, or the outfit?" replied a monotoned Zoe. I noticed a very un-Zóza expression had begun to creep steadily into her countenance.

"Why, the outfit, silly! Marcums said to go get myself something down at the Paseo Nuevo—so I did! It's quite couture . . . don't you think?" she asked, hoping for a little reassurance.

"It's very pretty, Marci," I said genuinely. "Very couture."

"Why, you are the very definition of 'couture!'" exclaimed Zoe, suddenly perking up.

My eyes open in surprise as, unbelievingly, I look at Zoe.

"Just look at you, all gussied up," Zoe went on. "Lil' Miss Marci 'Couture' Van der Kamp. You look like a great big bowl of genuine 'strutting down the boulevard' New York City couture."

My jaw open, I stare in awe as I wonder *what in the devil has got into Zoe.*

"You should start your own fashion line—Marci Van der Kamp and her new line: 'Kamp Couture,'" Zoe went on.

Then two things happened:

Marcy, extremely pleased with herself, said, "Really!? Do you really think so?" and proceeded to give us a little twirl.

I, however, immediately turned and walked out the studio to the parking lot, my face reddening from suppressing the laughter. I only hoped I could make it outside before it over-whelmed me. I thanked god my bladder was empty.

Zoe has said many funny things through our years together. But the timing of this was a masterpiece.

While for years having a perfect understanding of Dutch, Zoe had never spoken it. So when she actually started speaking Ukrainian with Nastya, I admit I was ever so slightly envious.

But, God as my witness, I never expected her first spoken Dutch words that day.

And in addition to being an on-the-spot improvisation, it was a private joke, just for me.

When Zoe said Marci looked "couture," she ever so subtly altered the pronunciation, and adjusted the stress.

In effect, what she actually said was not 'couture,' but the similar-sounding Dutch phrase *'kut hoer'* which—needless to say—*has an entirely different meaning.*

While she blended the sounds, not quite one or the other, it was enough for me to pick up on.

Zoe came out to the parking lot to find me leaning against the wall in stitches. My eyes were tearing up so much from laughing that I could barely even see.

"Happy birthday, Stevie!" she said, my laughter now infecting her as well.

We paused to breathe, thinking it had passed.

"Freddy would be so proud!" I said, and with that the giggles overtook us again.

And then everything was funny. Two grown women in full embrace standing in a parking lot wearing nothing but tutus and point shoes giggling hysterically was funny.

When Ash and Freddy poked their heads out the door to see what the commotion was about, it made us laugh even harder. That they looked at each other, shook their heads, and walked back inside was funnier still. When Ash and Freddy came outside again, I was sure I was going to break a rib.

"Just go!" yelled Freddy, starting to laugh contagiously himself. "You girls are done for the day."

"Agreed," added Ash, chuckling. "I think your usefulness has passed. Get out of here. *Go celebrate—shoo!"*

"Suppressing it as best we could, with red teary eyes, we walked back inside and grabbed our bags, not even bothering to change.

Mistaking hilarity for sadness, Marci said, "Is everything okay?"

"Zoe's just received some distressing news from Australia," I improvised. "We learned that her much-loved pet wallaby Jojo just passed away."

"Ohhhh, I'm so sorry to hear that," consoled Marci as she gave Zoe a hug. "When I was a little girl I had a guinea pig named Mrs Boinkers. She was narcoleptic and one day when I was playing with her she went to sleep in my lap and just never woke up. I was heartbroken when she died. Know it will pass, Zoe, just give it time." Marci sombrely looked at Zoe and nodded her head in knowing commensuration.

This time it was Zóza who had to walk out the studio holding her breath.

Coda

54
Zófaniéstya

Shortly thereafter, Zoe took Marci under her wing and began to develop her innate talent into something really special. Indeed, grooming her. And though she never mentioned it, and it sailed right past Marci, I knew my kind-hearted Zóza felt somewhat rueful by our improvised puns at Marci's expense on my birthday—*I certainly did.*

So, late on my birthday, after the evening's celebrations had wound down, while the boys were on the sofa, enjoying toasted brioche rounds with creme fraiche, caviar, and watching *The Notebook* . . .

Okay—"rigorous honesty" dictates: they were the couch, eating Doritos, and watching *Creepshow* . . .

Zoe and I went to my bedroom to have a little chat.

We spoke at length about my own trials and tribulations at CCB before she arrived, and how uncomfortable I had felt with all the animus that had been directed at me.

"Listen, Zóza," I posed rhetorically. "I mean, if Marci, on the one hand, feels a sense of entitlement and at the same time, is lacking self-esteem—what does that really make her?"

Zoe, seeing where I was headed, nodded in agreement. "A typical young artist—just like we were." Zoe reflected a moment longer before continuing. "So are we the ones acting superior now, Stevie? Maxwell Maltz says that a superiority complex is really just a ruse."

"Tell me," I encouraged.

Zoe closed her eyes for a moment, then opened them in that way that she does sometimes, eyes glancing upwards, darting slightly back and forth, as if examining something inside her mind.

"'People who seem to have one are actually suffering from feelings of inferiority; their "superior self" is a fiction, a cover-up, to hide from themselves and others their deep-down feelings of inferiority and insecurity.' And I have to agree—I've found that to be true in my life, anyway," she finished.

"Is that a quote from something?" I asked, intrigued. I've never asked Zoe to do parlour tricks—never wanted her to feel like she's my performing seal—but, as she brought it up—admittedly, I'm still as fascinated as the next person.

Zóza smiled sweetly. "Yeah, Stevie—page forty-three of *Psycho-Cybernetics*." She looks up and darts her eyes another second. "Tenth line of the third paragraph."

My gorgeous, gifted Zóza.

So after a bit more discussion, together, and with a decent dose of deference, Zoe and I agreed to put a stop to any further in-jokes regarding Marci—and before she really became aware of it (though honestly, at first, there were times we had to suppress the occasional glance at each other, as the inevitable eye-rolling which followed would have been simply unavoidable).

And going forward, from time to time we even made it a point to invite Marci to the occasional luncheon or join us on a shopping trip as an honorary member of our little "club"—which I would soon christen "Zófaniéstya." (Zóza-Stefanie-Connie-Nastya.)

Nastya, whom Marci idolised, gently explained that it might be seen as presumptuous to be giving advice to the more seasoned dancers in the company, but recognising her teaching ability, offered her a part-time job as an instructor at the newly opened, Moreton Bay Academy of Dance.

Marci and Marcus (henceforth known as *"M&M"*) eloped to Las Vegas one weekend only to return wearing a vaguely familiar ring.

Marcus did join the Board of Directors, by the way—and it was fine.

With a little time, Marci did begin to mellow, and I credit both Marcus and Nastya with having much to do with her maturation.

* * *

A few weeks later, Nastya and Connie arrived at the studio carrying in some boxes. Inside the larger ones were T-shirts bearing a silhouette of the Moreton Bay Fig Tree and the name of the company. A special one that Freddy had made especially for Zoe (an intentional size too small?) read on the back:

Balle-figgin-rina!
Fancy a fig?

It proved so popular with our theatre-goers that we ended up having to make a special order.

Another, smaller box, contained only four shirts. One for Connie, Nastya, Zóza, and me. Nastya and Connie excitedly informed us that on the front—if we were so inclined—*was to be the brand name of our new venture into fashion!*

Zófaniéstya!

And written higgledy-piggledy across the shirt in all the languages we collectively spoke was our company's provocative slogan:

A vindictive woman is worse than the devil.

"It's funny and irreverent and may put the fear of god into men . . . who will then placate their women by showering them with gifts—hopefully from us! That's the idea, anyway," Connie explained.

"It should get us on the map," Nastya added. "Besides, a little controversy is good for business. And by the way, we've already caught the interest of some investors."

Zoe and I were genuinely astonished! I knew not a whit about business—I had never done anything entrepreneurial in my life—but with Nastya's natural charm and business acumen and Zoe handling accounting and research, Connie and I were ready to lead the charge creatively.

55
The Feinting Lady

Initially it was thought that Ash and I would alternate leads with Freddy and Zoe; however, it soon became apparent that Freddy and Zoe had really made the parts their own, and Ash and I were but pretenders to the throne.

Instead, we played character roles of king and queen, and eventually, after much flattery, cajoling, wine, and treats, managed to persuade Bruce King to play the role of sword master.

We relieved "F&Z," as they came to be known, from as much administratively as possible so they could focus and recuperate.

As Bruce continued to work with Freddy and Zoe, it became apparent that they both displayed real talent with the blade, and not just stage talent. This allowed Bruce to increase the level of difficulty and speed of their encounters. This accorded with Ash's wish that the sword play be one of stylised realism.

Bruce, who was left-handed, but who could fence with

either hand, eventually switched to his left in order to further challenge Freddy.

This didn't work quite as well with Zoe, who simply also switched hands. However, Zóza's ambidexterity gave Bruce an idea: to have one scene where she, a foil in each hand, would fight opponents on either side of her simultaneously.

While this had done before, for ease, typically the same thrusts and parries are performed on each side at the same time. And indeed, this was originally the style of choreography Bruce planned for Zoe.

However, one morning before rehearsal, Bruce and I walked in the studio to find Freddy and Ash lifting their hands to halt and silence us. They, along with Nastya, Ambrose, Connie, and Pablo, seemed intently focused on something. Silently, they motioned us over, directing our attention to Zoe.

Zóza lay prone on the ground, *A Wrinkle in Time* propped open in front of her. In an open notebook, Zoe was challenging herself by translating contents of the book.

Writing in Dutch on the left-hand page, and Ukrainian on the right. A pen in each hand, Zoe was translating the book into both languages — *simultaneously.*

I laughed out loud. Silence wasn't necessary. I doubt a nuclear blast would have broken Zóza's concentration.

Zoe finished her page, rolled to her back, and, still holding her pens, slept for about five minutes. Then she got up and was Zoe again.

"I think Hebrew or Arabic would make it a little easier on the left-hand side," she remarked casually, passing us on her way to get some water. "It's written right to left, so transcribing would be more symmetrical."

"Well fuck me!" chuckled Freddy. "When you put it like that, *anyone could do it!*"

Bruce used this incident as a catalyst to choreograph swordplay with separate duals—and differently timed action— occurring simultaneously on either side of her. The clink of the blades fell in beautifully with the rhythmic syncopation of the music.

The action culminated magnificently with an aerial or butterfly jump: a sort of no-hands cartwheel that Zoe had learned for the scene. A foil in each hand, whilst parrying attacks on either side, she butterflies away at the last moment, causing her opponents to thrust their blades through each other instead.

Zoe relished the change of pace and the challenge of utilising a new dynamic movement vocabulary.

* * *

As the premiere of MBB's *The Feinting Lady* steadily approached, Ambrose was already busily choreographing *Neuken in de Keuken*. He intended it as short prelude ballet to be performed just before *The Nutcracker*.

While we had been calling it that unofficially around the studio, until I saw a mock-up of the actual program, I thought the title was only an in-house joke.

"Ambrose!" I exclaimed. "You can't possibly call it that!"

"Why ever not? If Willie can have his much *Much Ado*—why can't I have my *Neuken*?"

Ambrose was alluding to Shakespeare's play *Much Ado About Nothing*. The title of which—is in fact—a double entendre: "Nothing" as in gossip and tittle-tattle, of course; however, what many people don't realise is that "Nothing" (or "an O-thing") had another meaning, as well: *It's Elizabethan slang for a woman's privates.*

"You do know what *Neuken in de Keuken* means?" I implored.

"Listen, Stefanie," Ambrose pontificated, "you should know by now that I consider it a point of professional pride to remain blissfully ignorant in regard to all such trivial concerns—and besides," he inveigled, lowering is voice, *"how many Dutch speakers do we really have in Santa Barbara anyway?"*

"God help us all!" I chuckled to myself. And in that moment, it occurred to me that there was no place on earth I'd rather be than right here—and right now—surrounded by my people.

56
After

As it became clear to the Montecito Ballet, they had had a significant reduction in their funding—or more precisely, when it dawned on the dancers that their livelihood was at stake, many began to jump ship. And as it so happened, it was to our ship that many jumped.

Ash made good on his promise to give salaried positions to dancers who were willing to relocate from Seattle, and Ambrose even threw in travel expenses.

As Thomas Hargrove's choreography funding was cut by Montecito, and as he intended to set it on me anyway, he was welcomed by us at Moreton Bay with open arms.

Originally scheduled for a fall opening, for various reasons, life contingencies as it were, it needed to be delayed a year.

Nevertheless, Thomas arrived as originally scheduled and set the ballet on me. Zoe imprinted the choreography in that mind of hers, ready to retrieve it whenever required. As it turned out, it was over a year later, after which Thomas would again return to make possible adjustments and fine-tuning.

Mum became the president of the board, which proved an excellent fit, keeping her both busy as well as providing the two of us with some breathing space. Our relationship continued to improve as I both grew in my appreciation of her sacrifice for me, and as I more and more began to assert myself. She was also generous in her advice with my occasional question regarding Zófaniéstya.

Zoe and I, and now Serafina, for the time being retained our autonomy by keeping our flat on Anapamu. She was in most ways an ideal baby, though she would often stare at a hanging mobile for hours, the way most older children can stare at the television. She also began walking at seven months.

For their part, Ash and Freddy became flatmates again as well. And so it happened that it was often the case that one or another of us would awaken to find anything from an otherwise empty flat, to an overnight guest or two in the morning.

Freddy, of all people, became my go-to, when I found myself in certain predicaments, occasionally involving Mum, and usually of my own creation. He also became our unofficial flat captain.

As he said, we were, for the most part, "four people sharing a flat," and insisting on transparency at home as well as in rehearsals, right from the beginning, any potential fires were avoided, and small conflagrations were not allowed to smoulder; *speaking of which, both Ash and I quit smoking!*

Eventually, however, we decided enough was enough, and pooling our resources, the four of us purchased a fixer-upper

bed and breakfast a couple of streets up from our flat.
A place—*a real home*, where we all could continue to live
together, though with decidedly more space.

It was a lovely two-level old mansion complete with garden,
sunroom, a huge kitchen, and many extra bedrooms. Ash
and Freddy converted the downstairs living room into a
studio, making use of the thirteen-foot-high ceilings.

Jasper, once he had gotten over the initial shock, happily
took to exploring every niche and hollow. An elaborate
system of ladders and bridges that Ash built along the walls,
allowing Jasper vistas and vantage points from above, as
well as through-wall tunnels connecting the various rooms,
was especially appreciated. Though, just as often, he could
be found happily snoozing, snuggled up with Serafina.

Progress on the remodel proceeded smoothly with the
singular exception of what has since become known as "the
Ashammer Incident."

While Freddy had rented a nail gun, Ash was content doing it
old-school macho. And indeed, he was consistently driving a
sixteen-penny nail in flat in three or four swings: a tap or two
to set it, followed by two hard swings.

Proud of himself, and putting his balletic manliness on full
display, Ash nodded his head, grinned a "look at what your
man can do" grin, and started showing off by hammering
them in whilst looking at me.

By batting my eyes and tossing my hair, biting my lip and
otherwise unabashedly flirting with him, it is possible I was
complicit in his undoing. For following two consecutive
successes, his last swing landed full force on his finger.

Now, if I understand American vernacular correctly, Sebastian began yelling repeatedly at the top of his lungs for everyone in earshot to immediately commence with fornication.

I ran over to help—I didn't intend to laugh—and I mostly succeeded . . . mostly. I felt my "two out of three wasn't bad" comment, really helped to ameliorate the situation.

A few days later, I walked into the house to find Ash, finger still splinted, hanging a picture frame on the wall. He turned to me and squinted, twisted his lips to one side, said nothing, and went upstairs.

I walked over only to find that on the wall, in a small frame, finely decorated, mounted, and encased in glass, Ash had hung a twisted deformed nail. Below, engraved on the metal frame, in fancy calligraphic script, it bore the title *'Stefanie.'*

I smiled inwardly to myself before going upstairs in order to more properly attend to his injuries.

* * *

Freddy started the process of officially adopting Serafina, and began writing a novel based on his life dancing, struggles with addiction, and his eventual relationship with a magical creature known as Zoe.

He would often joke, "I'm a dancer and a now a writer—*of course I'm an alcoholic!"*

Freddy and Zoe also got officially engaged!

One quiet starlit night, overlooking the pacific, on the wind-swept bluffs of Santa Barbara, the four of us, along with

Ambrose, Nastya, Connie, Pablo, and Mum all in attendance, Zóza and I had our moonlight godmother ceremony after all. However, and much to the consternation of the boys, *the ceremony was not performed 'al fresco.'*

The intimacy of my relationship with Sebastian continued to grow, in both the teasing and the tactile. And as time wore on, more and more we found ourselves speaking indirectly of next steps.

57
The Mission

One day following morning rehearsals, I asked Zoe if she would like to take a walk with me. As Zoźa and I typically went everywhere together anyway, it was a slightly unusual request.

Zoe inclined her head to the side, and her soulful eyes searched me for a moment, making sure I was okay. "What are you thinking Stevie?" she asked.

We decided to take a walking tour of the Mission. And whilst ambling about the grounds, chatting away about the upcoming production, she inquired, "Stevie, I thought the plan was for me and Freddy to trade off leads with you guys, but looking at the dates on the calendar, the rehearsal schedule, it's all me and—"

"Zóza . . ." I interrupted, turning to face her. I looked in her eyes, and taking her hands in my own, I said, *"There's been a slight change of plan."*

Zoe raised an eyebrow as her penetrating eyes looked deep within me. A beatific Zóza smile began to slowly spread across her features. Her gorgeous brown eyes welled up and tears began to flow down her cheeks.

"Oh, Stefanie!" she cried.

I lifted Zóza hands to my lips and meeting her eyes, kiss them gently before placing them on my tummy—

"My dearest Auntie Zóza . . . I believe it's my turn to take a year off."

~ *The End* ~

Zófaniéstya photo shoot——Stefanie 01

Zófaniéstya photo shoot——Stefanie 02

~ Stefanie's Sonnet ~

The shield of my conviction torn asunder.
Veracity cracks and splinters its facade.
My cirrus lies of white darken with thunder.
Must my marrow be inherently so flawed?

I recklessly suspend my disbelief.
My fabric's thread so frayed I barely breathe.
Unfailingly, neglect leads one to grief.
Perhaps it's only me whom I deceive?

~

Then hearts and hands begin to intertwine.
Awakening——thy touch, I find thee near.
How hath thou tamed the chaos of my mind?
Wherefore thy presence so subdues my fear?

While ruin may rain upon me from above.
The tumult of my mind . . . hath learned to love.

~ Stefanie Soulier!

Afterthought

While never overtly stated within the confines of this novel, Stefanie, as you may have inferred, suffers from — *or perhaps is blessed with* — an undiagnosed case of cyclothymia, a type of bipolar disorder, formerly known more commonly as manic depression.

Sudden changes of mood, marked creativity, racing thoughts, and lack of sleep are all common characteristics of this condition.

Manifesting in her late teens, Stefanie had come to both think of, and accept herself, as extremely moody, or the term she prefers: "capricious."

"Stefanie may just be the The Silmarillion of ballet-themed romances."

About the Author

Warren Pierce initially rose to fame in his twenties by riding 'Porthos the Titmouse' to victory in the annual East Indies Pterodactyl race for which he received the Golden Lingam.

After winning the 2017 Florence Forster Jenkins Award for Literary Excellence in Acerbic Nonfiction, he published his AudioBooks for Dogs program™, to great acclaim, helping usher in a new era of canine eroticism.

Self-help titles include: *"Retaliation-ships: Moving from Sublimation to Subjugation," "Thinking Thoughts About Myself,"* and the wildly popular *"Misanthropy for Dummies."*

*   *   *

Technically a high school dropout, Warren left high school after his junior year with the intention of racing motorcycles. How he winded up dancing ballet is anyones guess. Clues suggest that a ten year old boy, he was drafted by his older sister as her partner in hour long kitchen disco dancing sessions—soon followed by line dancing, breakdancing, gymnastics, martial arts and mime.

Always having a wide variety of interests, over time, Warren observed his skill in any particular area to be inversely proportioned to the amount of books he had on the subject. i.e. Professional dancer, no books. Frustrated musician—hundreds.

Slowly, some soulful semblance of superstition saturated his sensibilities and situated itself singularly in his psyche: Theory bad. Dive in, figure it out for yourself, and find your voice, good—Theory will always be there waiting when you need it. Ballet—the 'theory' of dance, was discovered only well after he had learned much movement vocabulary on his own.

Therefore, other than eleventh grade high school English, no classes, workshops, writing retreats or how-to books were harmed in the drafting of this novel. The singular exception being one frayed, jagged eared copy of Stephen King's 'On Writing,'

He lives in Newcastle, WA.
(This is his first book.)

www.warrenpiercebooks.com

Zófaniéstya photo shoot——Stefanie 03

CPSIA information can be obtained
at www.ICGtesting.com
Printed in the USA
BVHW022311240122
627060BV00003B/34/J

9 781525 593383